I0631549

From Mafeking to Molehills - The Reluctant Cub Scout

Best Global Publishing
For your story to be read
For your voice to be heard

From Mafeking to Molehills

Published by:
Best Global Publishing Ltd
PO Box 9366
Brentwood
Essex
CM13 1ZT
United Kingdom

www.bestglobalpublishing.com

The Reluctant Cub Scout

The author wishes to thank the following, it would have been impossible without them. To Jenny and Robert who made it all possible, to Sarah, Beverley, Hillary and Vix who corrected my spelling along with the grammar and laughed in all the right places.

Also to Gerard, and Rob Smith my agent, who made it happen.

From Mafeking to Molehills

To Carolyn, my wife for thirty years; thank you.

From Mafeking to Molehills

About the Author

Jon Laidlaw is fifty four. Born, raised and educated in the village of Shepperton. The younger of identical twins. He is married to Carolyn and has two children James and Victoria. He now commutes between his homes in Marbella and Hampshire.

From Mafeking to Molehills

The Reluctant Cub Scout

The Law of the Jungle states that wolves must gather to look over the new wolf cubs of the pack, so that they will know them and take care of them when they see them in the jungle

As each young wolf is pushed into the circle, Akela, the great leader of the wolf pack, sitting high on the Council Rock, called, "Look at each cub o' wolves. Look well". At last it was Mowgli's turn and Mother Wolf pushed him into the circle where he sat playing with some stones in the moonlight. Akela did not even twitch an ear as he called, "Look well, o' wolves."

From
"The Jungle Book"
Rudyard Kipling

From Mafeking to Molehills

INTRODUCTION

"It's not funny James. What the hell do I know about camping?" Christ, it must be at least thirty years since my twin brother David and I marched off to the Isle of Wight with the Church Lads Brigade. We had only joined them because the uniform was far more fashionable than the ones offered by the other youth organisations of that time. I can still remember struggling up the gentle slopes of Bembridge in the bright August sunlight sweating profusely under the unbearably stiff collars and heavy serge. But our buttons were clean and our boots were polished and apparently that was what was important.

"But Mrs Cunliffe, I mean Akela, says they need helpers and anyway I stuck my hand up now so you've got to do it."
"Thanks James" I said, thinking of my excuses already.
"She'll ring you tomorrow to arrange a meeting so that you can meet all the other dads who were, er... have, volunteered".

From Mafeking to Molehills

CHAPTER ONE

The phone rang as predicted with a shrill of urgency that seemingly grew louder and louder the longer I left it.

"Mr Laidlaw?" more of a statement than a question.

"Who's speaking?" I replied, knowing full well who it was on the other end.

Akela's voice was distinctive to say the least. Even in the short time my children had been attending the school I had learnt to recognise her educated and well-spoken tones.

"It's Jenny Cunliffe, from the school," she said with an air of authority that came with the territory of being a headmaster's wife.

"Ah yes, James said you might be ringing. How can I help?"

"Well it's like this....." Akela went on to explain what was needed and requested that I pop along to meet her socially, and introduce myself to her husband Robert and some of the other parents who were going to camp.

The school building itself wasn't that imposing, but the situation and atmosphere I now found myself in were. I was terrified that by opening my mouth and saying something stupid, quite easy for me to do according to my wife, 1 would send my children's chances of ever becoming prefects or school captains crashing to the ground along with all the 'lead balloons.'

"Meet Mike Harrison" said Akela, "he's head of corporate something or other at Black and Decker."

'Great, this bloke could come in handy for a discount,' I thought as I shook his hand as firmly as I could, remembering what my father had told me about first impressions and strong handshakes. As I over zealously pumped his hand I tried to impress him with some topical small talk, if only to show him that I wasn't as damp as the hand he was shaking. Corporate skills in the middle of a ploughed field, probably not very useful I thought. But still, what do I know?

"Mike's coming with us to camp and has offered to look after you," Akela beamed "You know, show you the ropes and so on."

"Great. Can't wait!" I lied, realising that I was getting in just a little deeper than I wanted to. "What do I sleep in?" I muttered to the staring faces that occupied the room, completely out of my depth. "I don't possess a tent or anything," I said, sounding just a little panicky as I looked for a way out both physically and mentally. "Don't worry about that," replied Robert "we'll sort you out, old chap. Take it from me; you've got nothing to worry about." He chuckled as he busied himself in the background, no doubt thinking 'another lamb to the slaughter'.

As my alarmed expression grew, Robert obviously started to feel a little sorry for me and promptly walked over and placed a large reassuring hand on my shoulder and smiled as he shook my sweat soaked hand with the other. "Can you come down to the campsite with me on Thursday to put a couple of tents up?" he asked whilst simultaneously passing a sheet of paper containing a list of what the cubs should bring to camp, as if in confirmation of my fate.

Apparently this was normal practice so that the boys would have somewhere dry to shelter and store their kit if it were to rain when we arrived at the campsite on the first day. However, I suspect it was also a clever ploy to see who and what they had as a helper.
"Yah, love to," I said not very convincingly, "What time do we leave?" slowly resigning myself to what now seemed inevitable. No backing out now Jonnie Boy!

Thursday started badly. I had been unable to sleep properly due to nightmares about collapsing tents and screaming children. I was getting pretty wound up because I couldn't find anything hanging in my wardrobe that would be suitable to wear in a muddy field on what was, after all, to be my inauguration of tent erection.

Finally I settled for an old pair of green corduroy trousers that had somehow managed to shrink whilst hanging in the wardrobe. I matched them nicely with a turquoise cable knit jumper that had gained a bit in the length of the arms as if to compensate. It had been a present from my colour blind aunt and I was glad to be making use of it. Things were getting a bit fractious within our normally happy household, as I turfed out the entire contents of the shoe cupboard and then the loft looking for suitable footwear. Eventually I chose an old pair of white deck shoes usually reserved for my Spanish holidays.

I sneaked the day off work by phoning in sick with 'a little bit of a tummy ache', and headed off to the school an hour earlier than planned. This was done to prove to Robert and Akela that I was not only as eager as they were, which wasn't quite the truth, but also that I was going to be a reliable volunteer for this year's camp.

Still feeling guilty about fibbing to the office, and more than a little self conscious because of the ridiculous clothing I had selected in haste, Robert and I, after having made some final adjustments to our cargo, jumped into the car and headed down to the campsite at Great Yews.

Light drizzle fell from a grey marble sky as we travelled south west towards Salisbury on the A303. We were accompanied by the Cunliffe's three large dogs, four small tents and a smelly rented marquee that had been crammed into the back of Robert's trusty Volvo.

It wasn't long before the confines of the car which was slowly being filled with methane from the dogs, along with the hot air being forced through the vents in an effort to de-mist the windscreen, compounded the lack of sleep from the previous night. Within minutes of the start of our journey I was quickly brought to that beautiful peaceful state of slumber, with my thoughts and dreams drifting back to my childhood days and Bembridge.....

I had never really been away from home without my parents before, and I don't suppose, at ten, many children had. Within a few days of our excited arrival I found myself missing them like mad. The days were great; action packed adventures and full of fun with plenty to keep our little minds occupied and therefore out of mischief. The nights however, were beginning to turn bad.

From Mafeking to Molehills

Most of the boys who were sharing the tent were slightly older and just a little more seasoned than I was. Their fertile imaginations and subsequent discussions started to play havoc with my mind. Talk of vampire bats and poisonous spiders was not what this frightened little ten year old wanted to hear. My innermost fears were only heightened by the elaborate story of one of the boys in the brigade being forgotten by his next of kin and left behind on some previous camp. According to legend he starved to death whilst trying to escape the island, and was apparently heard to wander the camp site at night in search of food and his neglectful parents.

By the fourth evening of what was beginning to feel like a very long week, I had had enough and lost it! Panicking, thinking that I was never likely to see my family again and was surely to be left on the Isle of Wight forever, I started to rant and rave like the very unhappy bunny I was. Unable to sleep or put up with my noise and disruption any longer, a couple of the boys who were sharing the tent, got me dressed and carted me off to the sanctuary of what was loosely described as the 'hospital' tent.

I was truly grateful for the companionship and comfort of the friendly leader who had been dispatched from his nice warm bed to look after

The Reluctant Cub Scout

me. Perhaps he might adopt me if my parents did forget me I was thinking as he sympathetically spent most of the night trying to reassure me that I "would" see Mummy and Daddy again. He finally calmed most of my fears by fibbing about the post that would be arriving the next day, and with this in mind I managed to sob myself slowly to sleep. Daylight came and thankfully I felt a little better, having discovered the promised mail tucked under my pillow. The letter comprised a quickly scribbled note from my parents telling me not to worry and that they would see me at the weekend. The handwriting was a bit suspicious and the envelope had no stamp on it but at that point I really didn't care. Just the thought of seeing Mum and Dad again and the faint hope that I might get off the island was enough to keep me going. Apart from the inevitable mickey-taking from my twin brother, who, if the truth be known, probably felt as bad and home sick as I did, I managed to survive the rest of the longest week of my ten year old life, mentally unscathed.

It's with grateful thanks I remember the kindness and understanding shown by the leaders of that particular camp and that experience has never left me. Rest assured any ten-year-old cub standing freezing cold in the middle of a muddy field in the dead of night, screaming for his parents will always have my sympathy.

"Not far now," said Robert slightly louder than necessary tugging me back to reality. I jumped with a start, smiling at him as he watched me trying to recover my composure, slightly embarrassed at the dribble that had run down the side of my mouth.

"We just need to pop over to Chafyn Grove School to collect a few bits and bobs," he said, then started to smile as he informed me that this was where he had taken his first teaching job, and where a little later on he had met Akela.

Catching the glint in his eyes, I returned his smile as I tried to imagine Robert who was about six or seven years older than me with a mop of unruly hair, running around the school as a young house master in hot pursuit of Akela. Jenny was the assistant matron at the time, and I chuckled at the image of them sneaking off to each other's rooms in the dead of night for good old rumpy pumpy. Great I thought these guys just might be human after all!

We pulled into the drive at Chafyn Grove, which stood serenely in plush grounds of roughly five acres, surrounded by huge trees early in the colours of summer, with beautiful lawns comparable to the manicured fairways of Berkshire.

The appearance of the school, for someone who had spent his educational years at a sixties Secondary Modern was, to say the least, impressive. I felt slightly out of place as I surveyed the various halls and classrooms as we passed by, but welcomed Robert's commentary on its long and illustrious history. I started to grow a little uneasy as I glanced at the numerous portraits of previous masters that hung from the panelled walls in the grand dining hall. Portraits of accomplished academics long since gone that seemed intent to follow my every move. Their inquisitive stares fixed me with unblinking eyes. They silently asked my learned companion who was the unworthy intruder he had carelessly brought into their school.

Thankfully as Robert continued the tour the atmosphere grew visibly lighter as we strode purposefully towards a slightly more modern set of buildings. These had apparently been added just a few years ago and turned out to be the gymnasium and where, during the half term holiday the tents we were to borrow had been sorted and stored.

From Mafeking to Molehills

The school's caretaker, who by the look of his stoop had probably been there as long as the original building itself, greeted us with a lopsided grin that had been caused by palsy or a stroke. With asymmetrically balanced eyebrows his shock of white hair and craggy complexion only enhanced the impression that I had just bumped into Quasimodo. The boiler suit he was sporting hung from his shoulder by a single strap, either to make some sort of fashion statement or more likely to advertise the fact that he was far too busy to dress himself properly. The garment itself was so badly faded and covered by such an assortment of stains (most of them of dubious origin) that it was hard to distinguish what had been its original colour.

"We'll take the hundred and fifty pounders," Robert shouted to the back of the caretaker's head as the old man shuffled off in the direction of a broom cupboard. Curiously enough it had 'Private, Caretaker's Office' scribbled in chalk on the door and was now partially closed against prying eyes as if he had something to hide. He managed to busy himself long enough for us to take the hint and Robert and I shrugged our shoulders and wandered over to the tents that had been neatly stacked awaiting their imminent collection.

The Reluctant Cub Scout

"Is the hundred and fifty pounds the cost?" I enquired; glad to be making intelligent conversation in such an intellectual place.

"What!" Robert replied shaking his head, and looking at me as if I had just crawled out of one of the jock straps hanging on the wire pegs over by the showers.

"It's the bloody weight of the canvas you idiot, not the price".

"Oh the weight!"......... The weight. Christ, I thought. I've got to hump these things two hundred yards to the car.

"Welcome to camping!" he smiled, as he caught my expression and then promptly hoisted one of the tents onto his shoulder with consummate ease and steadily marched off towards the Volvo.

In silence I surveyed the mountainous pile of canvas bags that lay before me and selected the smallest bundle I could find. Spitting on my hands I rubbed them together, strongman fashion, before wiping the uncomfortable residue down the back of my trousers. Taking a deep breath, I counted to three and started to tug.

I'd only been at this lark a couple of hours and was completely knackered already. I had to keep reminding myself that if the British Army could run up and down mountains whilst carrying these things strapped to their backs, seemingly for fun, then wimpy boy here could manage to carry one to the car park. Doggedly I started to drag the thing, inch by inch, down the gravel path whilst trying to ignore not only Robert's comments each time he hurried past but the sniggering laughter from the man in the broom cupboard. It wasn't until later that we found that I'd managed to wear a hole big enough to stick my arse through the only tent I had actually managed to take to the car, rendering completely useless some of the finest army surplus money could buy. Eat your heart out Hitler!

CHAPTER TWO

For me Saturday, the first day of camp came with all the anticipation and trepidation of an execution. Although I was packed and ready to go, I was not fully prepared mentally. For comfort I reverted to the list Robert had given me on our very first meeting and kept continually checking that I hadn't missed or forgotten anything essential. Silly really, because I had naively adhered to the instructions to the letter, and had barely packed anything at all, telling myself I should only take what was on the list.

I had spent the previous week swatting over an SAS survival manual that had been loaned to me by a wag at work. I wasn't at all confident that I could survive five days and four nights with only 1 blanket; 1 sleeping bag; 1 kit bag; 2 woollen jumpers (not synthetic); 2 T-shirts (not football type); 3 pairs socks; 3 pairs pants; 2 pairs jeans and washing kit. In hindsight the latter was pointless as with most of the cubs', it never saw the light of day. But it was all a little late now.

As we set off we left behind lots of tears from heartbroken parents. Most of them convinced that they would never see their precious babies again. Or perhaps they were tears of joy at finding cheap baby sitters for the half term holiday week. Who knows? Anyway, we madly waved our goodbyes through the open windows of the mini buses and eagerly started our journey in what could loosely have been described as a convoy. Fully laden and with happy hearts we slowly trundled south westwards towards Salisbury, Great Yews and our campsite.

I had been given the job of driving one of the minibuses. Not quite what I was used to, however. I have been fortunate over the years and was at that time driving some of the finest German engineering manufactured. This thing had been made just outside Luton and handled like the beast it was. That's to say a minibus with the top speed of a rampant slug, unpredictable, uncontrollable and full of bouncing children. Miraculously, after having spent two hours second guessing the steering wheel, twenty minutes stopping for pee breaks and two more for the inevitable disposal of sick bags, we somehow managed to arrive safely at our destination.

Great Yews was magnificent! A giant yew tree forest that completely surrounded the campsite we were to use. Lush and green and totally secluded it settled nicely into the backdrop of

the Wiltshire countryside just a few miles south
of Salisbury.

Its soft springy grass was kept short by the
sheep that were allowed to graze freely in the
area and complimented the startling dense
foliage that grew flat along the yew tree
branches a couple of meters from the ground,
giving a very vivid and visual effect, similar to
that of permafrost.

The contradictions between the hard gnarled
and twisted trunks that spiralled slowly
skywards before disappearing into an
elaborately soft but solid ceiling of the lush
green canopy was stunning. With shafts of
bright sunlight that stabbed their fingers
through the feathered branches as if pointing
the way into the deep and darkened forest
towards some strange foreboding land. This
was a fairy tale place found only in the
storybooks we read as children. Tales of lost
youngsters and little old ladies baking
gingerbread. Just about the right atmosphere
for camping cubs, I thought.

Great Yews was at one time owned and used by
the Earl of Radnor. Apparently he would send
his family down to the hunting lodge that was
situated within the grounds of Great Yews
during times of strife. You know the sort of
thing, The Plague, Black Death, and Famine.

From Mafeking to Molehills

Pretty convenient by all accounts, but only available to the lucky few.

Surprisingly the hunting lodge still stands, considering it was made completely of wood. It had been frequently used by the scouting association for many years, and had witnessed more camp fires than a Greenham Common girls' night in. Still, there was plenty of time left as 10th Camberley hadn't finished with it yet. The lodge nestled snugly to the right hand side of the camp site as you entered and was to be used as a 'dry shelter' for the duration of our stay. Compulsory when camping with young children, handy really, I thought, and the first place I'd go if it all became too unbearable...

It had been raining for most of the previous week and the lane that approached Great Yews was decidedly boggy. It was certainly not capable of taking minibuses laden with cubs, or a van full of camping equipment. So after explaining the ancient proverb to the boys about many hands and all that, we formed a human chain and busied ourselves with the job of unloading the equipment we were to use that week.

To this day it still amazes me how quickly things get done and how eager ten-year-olds can be. Little scraps heaving and tugging at things twice their size, seemingly impervious to the effects of the sore back and pulled muscles that had already besieged my body.

With every stabbing pain I was reminded of how completely out of condition I really was and had to gently remind myself that if I wanted to survive this camp I would have to be very careful every time I bent down. Even if it were only to lift a tent peg!

Apparently, the secret of camping was to pace oneself. Mike Harrison had preached this to me as we unloaded the van. Great advice but it was very nearly impossible to implement with thirty five cub scouts running riot around a yew tree forest. Regardless of how many "helpers" were around, I felt personally responsible for all of them. Constantly observing, mostly with my heart in my mouth as I desperately tried to make sure that no harm came to our charges.

If the truth be known it was me that needed protecting, and just to make the point, a group of cubs casually wandered up to me with something cupped in one the older boy's hands. "Look what I've found!" he said smiling innocently, searching for my response.

"What have you got there?" I inquired suspiciously.

"I'm not sure Mr Gaylord, but you can have it."

From Mafeking to Molehills

"It's Laidlaw," I said as he tossed the contents towards me and watched in glee as the wriggling serpent plopped into my open palm.

Now I'm not particularly squeamish, but I defy anybody not to jump sky-high when someone dumps a snake into your hands without warning. To be truthful, if I hadn't been in the middle of a field with ninety three million miles of headroom, I would have banged my head.

"Ugh! It's a snake!" I screamed as I dropped it.

"No, it's not Mr Gaylord. It's only a slow worm, it won't bite" he laughed, as he scampered off to his mates who all stood in a gaggle and giggled giving each other 'high fives' and turned in unison as they made a 'one up to us' sign.

"It's Laidlaw", I said "and there's a bloody good chance I might" I shouted a little too loudly as I watched in disbelief as the legless lizard, as it was correctly known, slithered off in the direction of my tent.

I instantly regretted the move as soon as I had made it. But in my defence the reaction was made instinctively and in truth the poor creature probably didn't feel a thing as it disintegrated under the impact of my boot.

"Bloody hell" I screamed as I hopped round in circles trying to flick the residue off my foot.

"Ugh! Gross!" shouted one of the boys who had been standing in the circle and was now looking on in horror as he witnessed my intolerance to wildlife.

"Someone call the RSPCA" his mate shouted, "Mr Gaylord's a murderer."

"Yes, yes I'm sorry" I said hoping that this wasn't going to be reported to Akela. "It's Laidlaw and I didn't mean to do it, it was a sort of accident."

"O yeh, some accident" said the obvious ring leader who pointed to the blood covered debris that was now hanging lifeless from the side of my tent, "like you didn't mean it."

"Yes well, run along and do something useful," I said trying not to show my annoyance.

"What like get a cloth?" he sniggered.

"Very funny" I said. "Now bugger off."

After watching the boys saunter off towards another crowd of cubs no doubt to tell them in exaggerated gory detail what Mr Laidlaw had just done, I wiped the congealing mess from the canvas and walked hurriedly away from the crime scene. Chastising myself for my lack of self control both physically and verbally I silently promised to try and do better the next time and went to seek solace in a much safer place.....somewhere behind Akela's skirt.

After four gruelling hours, camp had been set up. Taking stock and a well-earned rest I surveyed the handy work. I was impressed with how tidy it all looked. Everything had its place. The provisions had been packed into the store tent, all additional kit and tools into the supply tent, and thirty-five cubs into theirs.

The only blot on the landscape was this very sad looking object disguising itself as my tent. It had been tucked somewhat suspiciously as far away from the main camp as was possible, a little to the right of the store tent just in front of the entrance gate.

"We've put you down there by the store tent Jon, as guard," said Robert as he once again put a reassuring hand on my shoulder and shepherded me towards my digs. "For security purposes, you understand - just in case."

"Just in case of what?" I thought out loud. I'd never done anything like this before as a grown up, and now, having been tainted with all the horrors of the world, I started to imagine all sorts of crazy things. What would I do if *this* happened? What would I do if *that* happened? Blimey if they expect me to guard and protect them then we are all in trouble. I've already shown them how brave I am with the snake thing.

Night had closed in fast as it does when you are unable to illuminate the world by suddenly switching on a light. And it was at this time I started to realise how far we humans have come. Not always such a good thing but nevertheless how reliant and utterly dependent we are on modern technology and how difficult life would be without it. There I was wandering around the camp in total darkness looking for my kit bag. I hadn't seen it since our arrival and was fumbling around with a box of matches trying to shed some light on the situation, managing in the process to step, slip and slide blindly into most of the deposits left by the previous grazing tenants of the field.

Apparently my kit bag had been mistaken for one of the children's and because no one had claimed it, been unceremoniously slung into the supply tent along with all the other surplus equipment. I finally found it buried under the unusable tent I'd managed to damage a few days earlier and searched in desperation for the torch I'd forgotten to pack. All because it wasn't on the list!

After the final checks to make sure the boys were asleep and that none had managed to escape, the 'adults' as Akela liked to refer to us, filed into the small wooden hunting lodge for refreshments and a well deserved sit down. We parked ourselves around the magnificent fire that had been expertly stoked by Mike Harrison.

From Mafeking to Molehills

Gingerly we forced ourselves into some flimsy canvas fold away chairs that you normally take on picnics. Chairs that should, in everybody's opinion, especially Robert's, be left as far away from any proper camp site as possible.

We started discussing our plan of attack for the days ahead, and as the evening wore on, the welcome coffee and brandy supplied by Robert began to take effect. With the efforts of the day comfortably behind us, we all started to relax a little more and enjoy the hospitality being offered. Basking in the warmth and comfort of the fire, we all slowly started to unwind.

Mike Harrison was a large slightly overweight man of about my age, probably slightly older, or maybe he was just wearing badly. His bloodshot eyes surrounded by heavy bags that hung from dark sockets told of busy schedules and very late nights. His hounded expression of permanent tiredness etched deep into the lines of a face that had once been handsome. He was now let down by the tobacco stained grin and hair that was prematurely greying, confirming the strains of corporate life.

Anyway, having been the previous year he was certainly more experienced than I was in the noble art of cub camping and just to prove this point he had brought along with him copious amounts of kit. Included in his 'Necessary and Essential Equipment', along with most other things, was a magnificent sheathed knife.

Mike had been donning this thing all day long. Apparently it was capable of skinning a buffalo at fifty yards or something, and he was wearing it strapped around his waist, slung low, and gunfighter style. Just a little over the top for a cub camp I thought, but whatever. Anyway, as Mike began to lean back to assist the fourth or fifth very large brandy to descale the Salisbury dust from his throat, he slowly stretched backwards to relieve his aching limbs that were now tiring quickly at the end of what had been a very long working day.

From that moment onwards, science took over. Simply beautiful to watch and even better to laugh at, as he lost his equilibrium. Slowly he passed that wonderful point of no return; you know that point of balance we've all experienced as youngsters in the school classroom. That seemingly endless moment when you know that gravity has taken over and regardless of how many times you waggle your legs or what ridiculous movements you make, you're not going to swing the scales of balance back in your favour. Feeling helplessly stupid, you know inevitably that you are going to fall flat on your back, and sure enough, he did.

From Mafeking to Molehills

Bewildered by the noise, the others looked round to see what the commotion was, only to see poor Mike Harrison laying flat out making silly little jerky movements and moaning.

"Help I think I've broken my back." Apparently unable to stand up, he was crying "I can't move. Help! Somebody please help me, oh, ouch, oh, I'm paralysed."

Horrified, we all rushed to his aid, worried that we might already have our first serious casualty of the cub camp, discounting the cut fingers on three different cub scouts the minute that the Swiss army penknives came out. Funny that, I didn't think Switzerland had an army, but apparently, they have. Anyway, Mike was still yelling at the top of his voice.

"Help me. I mean it, I can't move. Call an ambulance, hurry. I can't get up."

After watching this charade for a couple of minutes I suddenly realised that he was unable to move because his buffalo killer, namely his oversized sheath knife, had wedged itself between the collapsed arm and leg of the chair. Regardless of what he tried to do he couldn't get up whilst lying on the chair. As it slowly dawned on us that he hadn't actually hurt himself, fuelled by the relief as well as the alcohol, we all started to fall about laughing.

The Reluctant Cub Scout

Once we had managed to undo his belt and release the knife from the vice-like grip of the chair, no mean task at that, we gently heaved him upright. After brushing himself down, and unable to hide the embarrassment from his less than manly display, he made his apologies and stumbled out of the lodge and disappeared across the field towards his tent. Accompanied, I must add, by the sniggering of the rest of the adults.

He stopped only when it became impossible for him to walk any further without pulling his trousers up from around his knees.
"A bit of street cred lost there, old chum," I laughed unable to hide my pleasure. Needless to say the knife wasn't seen for the rest of the camp.

CHAPTER THREE

After an earlier rain shower, the night was now clear, giving its warning of the cold to come. With the black velvet sky offering more diamonds than De Beers, it reminded me once again of how much we miss whilst living in the towns and cities we call suburbia. As long as man walks this planet I thought, songs and poems would be written about starry nights like these.

Tired and exhausted I stumbled down the field towards my tent with soaking wet feet, having failed to avoid the various booby traps of buckets of water the older boys had set out just for me. I fumbled into my tent and proceeded to zip it up. First the outer canvas, then the inner tent, and after deciding that it was a little too parky to fully undress, I took my wet shoes and socks off and sat cross legged on the ground sheet. Crouching forward so that my head didn't touch the wet sagging canvas, I tried to dry my feet as best I could in total darkness by using my one and only jumper. I then wriggled into my sleeping bag and zipped it up as far under my chin as possible, lovely and snug.

Within a few minutes I began to realise that the cold was starting to creep up from my toes and was now proceeding menacingly towards my head. Regardless of how exhausted I felt, it was impossible to sleep. Not only because it was unbelievably uncomfortable lying directly on the ground, but because I couldn't stop my teeth from chattering.

I lay awake and tried to remember if the ground at Bembridge had ever been this hard and stared at the canvas that was now almost touching my nose as it bulged menacingly with the collection of earlier rainfall. My tedium was only broken by the clouds of condensation that puffed from my mouth before settling on the metal frame above. Each time I exhaled, a droplet of ice cold water would bounce off my forehead. By three in the morning I had reached my lowest ebb. The coffee and brandy so eagerly consumed the evening before had managed to work its way through my system and was knocking impatiently at the door of my bladder. Even though I kept convincing myself that I didn't want to go, I did.

I was now very reluctant to leave the relative warmth of my sleeping bag having successfully generated a little heat by continuously spinning round inside it in an effort to find a soft spot on what was now frozen ground. I lay there in discomfort for another hour before the pain became too unbearable and rational thinking took over. And so the ritual of the zippers began. A ritual, I might add, that I performed every single night of cub camp.

It went something like this. First unzip the sleeping bag, unzip the inner tent, unzip the outer tent, unzip the fly, pee, zip up the fly, zip up the outer tent, zip up the inner tent and so on. Anyway having relieved myself and feeling much better, I snuggled down for what was left of my first night of cub camp.

"Cuckoo!"
"Cuckoo!"
"What the Hell?"
"Tweet Tweet,"
"Tweet Tweet"
Welcome the dawn chorus.

There I was, in the middle of a field surrounded by woods. My limbs were numb and aching from sleeping on the ground without a mattress (yet another mistake I had made). Having had no sleep at all, freezing cold, stiff, sore and decidedly irritable from being kept awake by some bizarre water torture; I was now being greeted by thousands of twittering birds telling me how wonderful life was. Quite unbelievable...and frankly, and I quote, 'not the best preparation for tackling the day with thirty five cub scouts'.

The Reluctant Cub Scout

"It's five o'clock in the morning" I said to myself as I glanced in disbelief at my wristwatch.

"Yea, good in't it Mr Lay-lord," said an enthusiastic cub as he poked his head into my tent, in an attempt to discover who or what would live in such a dilapidated state.

"It's Laidlaw," I said not too happy with the early morning alarm call, still wondering how I had managed to drop my guard long enough to get talked into volunteering. But his smiling sunny face and the thoughts of all the wonders that lay ahead of me on my second day of cub camp started to lift my sprits slightly.

Gingerly I climbed from my 'pit' so as not to disturb the puddles of frozen rainwater that had pooled nicely in the sagging canvas and meticulously stepped over the guys that were now stretched so taut that they were creaking from the weight. I made a mental note to try and adjust the tent before going to bed that night but then decided not to fix what wasn't broken, always a good policy where I was involved.

Enjoying the fresh clean air of the early morning I wandered around until I found Mike Harrison 'brewing up' on yet another snazzy piece of equipment.

From Mafeking to Molehills

"Tea old boy?" he said, seemingly over the embarrassment of the previous night and I smiled in sympathy as I remembered the fiasco. "Um! Yes please" I said, desperately in need of something warm to re-align my frozen thoughts.

"How'd you sleep?" he smiled, knowingly knowing that the chance of anybody without his style of SAS equipment having had a wink of sleep were nil.

"Great, super, no problems," I lied through gritted teeth, this being the only way I could stop them from chattering in the cold morning air.

"Oh that's good," he mumbled as he searched my face for any evidence of deceit. "We need to do some digging over there," he nodded and marched off, cup in hand, to find Robert who had been up for hours and was already knee deep in what looked suspiciously like a grave.

Maybe something or somebody hadn't made it through the night, I was thinking or perhaps the dogs had killed a sheep or wild animal or even worse, a cub! Well at least I'm not the only guilty one I thought as I wandered over as slowly as I could towards where the others were working. Christ! I hadn't realised how dangerous this camping lark could be, and certainly didn't want to start my second day in camp as some unlawful gravedigger and be dragged into this terrible conspiracy. Not because of the hard manual work, you understand, but because I didn't think it was ethical to bury some poor little cub or whatever without the blessing of the parents.

I stood back to allow the others to do the dirty deed and watched as they heaped shovels full of the dark rich soil into mountainous piles that obscured my view. Finally they stopped and I was semi grateful that the hole they had been digging was only large enough for one small cub.

"Do you think this is right?" I said, not sure I should speak my mind at such an early stage of my camping career.

"How do we explain this?" I said as I waved my hand across the hole in the ground hoping that it might give them a pang of conscience.

"What on earth are you going on about?" sighed Robert as he looked around for confirmation from the others that he was dealing with an idiot.

"What do we tell the landowner or farmer?" I said in the hope it wasn't a cub. "You know, about this grave thing," as I pointed to the oblong shaped trench nestling nicely under one of the yew trees.

"A very nice spot under the dappled shade and all that, but"...

"Somebody hit him with a spade," said Robert as he walked away slowly shaking his head.

"It's not a grave you clot! It's called a latrine," Mike chuckled "although if it were a grave, I can think of somebody who could make very good use of it."

The relief on my face was visible as Robert returned corpse-less holding a bottle of foul smelling chemical and proceeded to pour the dark blue contents into the trench. He assured me that this was the place where the latrines, toilets in other words, would be emptied during our stay at camp and suggested that I should stay as far away from it as possible.

"Not only is it dangerous, but it smells," said Robert who had already made up his mind that if anybody could fall headlong into a shit tip, Jonnie Boy would.

CHAPTER FOUR

There is something sad and pathetic about a thirty-five year old man traipsing around like a lost puppy. But there I was, aimlessly wandering about, completely clueless, latching onto anybody who happened to saunter past. So much so that Akela finally got fed up with all the complaints about me getting in the way and suggested somewhat tactfully that I should go and do something useful with the cubs. Anything as long as it got me from under their feet. So with these instructions I grabbed an old tatty football from the store tent and a well bitten whistle that was kept in the first Aid box stored in the glove compartment of the minibus and took the boys off to play football.

"Where should we go?" shouted one of the cubs who had been running ahead, punting the slightly deflated football skywards until it had landed in the chest high nettles that edged most of the campsite. He was now walking back towards me with his hands in his pockets having abandoned the football to some one else who was madly hopping around the stinging nettles with a large lump of rotting wood trying to fish it out
"I don't know. Try the woods," I said unable to think of anywhere more suitable that hadn't already been taken up with tents.

From Mafeking to Molehills

"You're mad," he replied shaking his head from side to side either in pity or disbelief.

"Yes, you're probably right," I laughed, as I wondered what on earth I was doing here.

Silly as it sounds, cub football in a yew tree forest is possible. The tree canopy as described before was about six feet off the ground and with the cubs being no more than four-foot tall, there was ample headroom. The trees were spaced roughly twenty to thirty feet apart so, provided you learned to miss them, play was just about manageable. The foliage underfoot was deep from many years of leaf fall, forming a sumptuous cushioned ground that made it very nearly impossible to hurt yourself if you fell. Now provided you looked where you were going, and didn't bump into the odd tree or two, the place was very nearly perfect. Avoiding these obstacles was not always possible when you're hurtling headlong down the pitch, dribbling the ball on one of those mazy runs like Ryan Giggs. But all in all, the woods made for a tremendously enjoyable game of football.

The Reluctant Cub Scout

Inevitably, after various rows and side swapping, along with the ever-increasing shouting from the disagreements about my poor refereeing decisions, the noise levels began to rise. Bearing in mind that I'd had very little sleep and was suffering from a thumping headache brought on by the stress and constant fear of being thrown out of cub camp for being so useless, I decided to bring into play the rules of silent football.

Wonderful! Instant peace! Can you imagine a whole gaggle of eight, nine and ten year old boys bursting at the seams, desperately wanting to call, shout and scream at their team mates in an attempt to gain the ball, only to be sent off instantly if they so much as made a squeak. I don't think I've ever seen such discipline and self-control in my life. It was brilliant.

However, having entered the woods with thirty plus boys making enough noise to wake the dead, or whatever lurked within the depths of this forest, you can understand the reactions of the rest of the camp staff when suddenly everything went quiet.
"What's going on?" called Robert trying not to show too much concern.

"Nothing," I shouted "just changing the rules a little" I laughed, and with the smile still etched on my face went back to being the most hated referee in football.

When a whistle is blown at camp (other than when playing football) everything stops immediately. No ifs, ands, or buts, you drop whatever you are doing and return to the flagpole. This rule is written in stone; for obvious reasons one of these assemblies was called each morning followed by a 'Roll Call.' With this done, Akela would then explain the program of events for that particular day.

With this being our first full day at camp the boys were told that as we would be cooking on open fires for most of our meals, weather permitting, firewood would have to be collected. So armed with this instruction the cubs scattered in all directions whooping and making banshee noises as they disappeared into the forest in search of wood.

Robert, Mike Harrison and I commandeered the saws from a couple of the bigger lads who were protesting that they were far more capable than some of the present company, no name's mentioned.

The Reluctant Cub Scout

"You're probably right," said Robert "but rules are rules and saws can be dangerous and therefore should only be handled by a responsible adult."

"So why is he touching one?" smirked Mike Harrison as I proceeded to haphazardly attack whatever the boys dragged back from the scavenging.

Tirelessly we worked cutting the lumber into manageable pieces, content with our labours as we chatted and joked about the previous night's mishaps. As the search for decent wood became more and more difficult, the pieces being brought back to us were beginning to get larger and larger. We, on the other hand, were getting weaker and weaker. Thankfully Robert called a halt when half a dozen cubs emerged from the woods carrying what could only be described as a tree complete with leaves.

He tactfully suggested that they should all start collecting 'kindling'. This apparently is the little scrappy bits and pieces that get the fire started, and to be honest I was very grateful for the rest. I sat back on the log pile and licked the enormous blister that had appeared on my hand as soon as I had started cutting the wood. Either I had missed out on the allocation of gloves when we had first grabbed the equipment or more likely had stepped over my pair in my enthusiasm.

This wasn't the first time I had suffered pain as a 'Lumberjack' and remembered with some embarrassment when my wife Carolyn and I bought a new house on the Surrey/Hampshire borders a few years back. Although the house was modern, it had a real open fireplace. Quite a novel feature apparently according to the estate agents blurb, anyway Muggins here, always in favour of saving a few bob, suggested we pop over to the local 'forest' and chop up some trees for firewood. You know 'Little House on the Prairie' style.

So, very early one bright December morning we wrapped ourselves up against the cold of the day and set off in search of suitable lumber. We equipped ourselves with an old rusty hand held axe that I had managed to find in among the cobwebs at the back of our garden shed and a couple of plastic carrier bags that we made the children carry. One stuffed full of goodies to be used as bribes along the way, for even at this early stage my reluctant children were protesting that their feet were cold and were exhausted at having to get up at the crack of dawn, and it wasn't even a school day!. The other was to be used to carry our firewood if we were successful.

The Reluctant Cub Scout

Even with my limited knowledge of survival, I knew that green wood didn't burn. We walked for mile upon mile, bribe upon bribe in search of anything that might just ignite. Well it was slowly becoming obvious that not only was it very nearly impossible to find anything that wasn't still alive. When I did manage to trip up or stumble over some rotting branch or tree stump, the rebound from every ineffectual strike of the axe would send shock waves screaming through the handle and straight up my arm. Apparently I had an inadequate chopper according to my wife who was smirking some distance away whilst trying to protect the children from my flailing arms. Clouds both physically and mentally started to appear as it soon became apparent that if left to fend for myself, lost in some dark deserted woodland somewhere north of Basingstoke, I would probably die in about ten minutes.

Disillusioned, disheartened and just a little sore, I suggested sheepishly to Carolyn and the kids that it might just be the wrong season for wood and that we might be more successful if we called into the local petrol station's mini market on our way home.

From Mafeking to Molehills

Log-less, and with my credibility at zero we traipsed back to the car and trundled off towards the nearest garage. Sure enough, there it was bundles and bundles of the wretched stuff in pre-packed bags stacked neatly on the forecourt, all waiting and willing to be burnt, and not a bloody splinter in sight. Sometimes I wonder.

The arrangements for cooking and eating at camp were such that the cubs were split into groups. Each group consisted of six cubs and these 'sixes' were given the name of a woodland animal, such as Squirrel, Badger, Donkey and so on.

Each six would be allocated an adult who would act as a supervisor and guest for that day's cooking. These adult helpers would then award points and mark the group they were with. The adult would move to a different six the next day. The points were awarded on the quality of food preparation and behaviour. These were totalled up at the end of camp and the winning six would be awarded a shield. This made for great competition and some of the boys took the acquisition of these points very seriously indeed.

The Reluctant Cub Scout

My education concerning eight and nine year olds started here. Their capability in preparing, cooking and serving edible tasteful food on an open fire astounded me. Quite frankly it completely altered my perspective on children. From being those useless, annoying little sods that only want you for pocket money and a personal taxi service, they transformed into willing eager learners who thoroughly enjoyed the challenge of preparing not only their own but also the adults' meals.

However, they say for every up there is a down, and the down side of cooking on open fires in camp is the washing up. Everything gets blackened, and cleaning the charred utensils is an almost impossible task. An even harder job however, was to convince the cubs of how much hot water they had to boil to complete this particular task.

This concept was especially difficult for those children who, up until two days beforehand, couldn't have found the kitchen at home without instruction let alone washed up in it. The closest most of these lads would get to washing up would have been to throw a few plates into the dishwasher, press a button and walk away.

From Mafeking to Molehills

Sadly with these reluctant helpers, washing up and clearing away after cooking could take forever, and eventually we would have to resort to bribery in an effort to complete the job. We promised them that if they finished in time we would play a wide game or something before cocoa, prayers and bed. This would usually do the trick and by late evening most things would be cleaned and stowed away. After checking a few suspicious 'Billy Cans' that still contained the odd slimy Brillo pad, we would gather around the flagpole whilst listening to Robert's instructions on what rules applied to which ever game we were about to play.

CHAPTER FIVE

Any body who has ever been blessed with children will tell you that they are quite capable of eating you out of house and home. With hollow legs and cavernous tummies they seem to grow like cuckoos, with permanently open mouths that get wider and wider in the relentless demand for food. And regardless of how many times you fill them up, your crisp cupboards and biscuit tins are always empty. Then they turn into teenagers with even larger appetites, and even bigger mouths.

Our only saviour is that, thankfully nearly everything these days is manufactured in convenience packaging. There is a price to pay, of course, and the price for this convenience is the huge amount of rubbish it generates. There is generally more wrapping than content. This is particularly true of cub camp and it wasn't long before mountainous piles of black bin bags started to obscure the horizon. This was not only becoming a health hazard but was inviting the wild and unwelcome woodland neighbours from all around the campsite.

Action needed to be taken and pretty quickly. So early one morning, Akela and I, having loaded the trailer with copious amounts of smelly black bags, set off with the intention of dumping them somewhere on our travels.

We were on our way to find a telephone box. This was prior to the invention of the mobile telephone, we needed to report back home that all was well, and that no ghosties had dragged us away during the cold frosty nights. The report was done so that worried parents could telephone into a central number and get any updates on the health and happiness of their precious little monsters.

We drove through several towns and small villages. All with there quaint little thatched roof cottages resembling the setting of a Constable painting, and whistled along the narrow lanes with their high hedgerows edged with Foxglove and buttercup as we continued our search for the illusive telephone. Eventually we passed through the counties of Wiltshire, Dorset, Somerset and back through Dorset in the vain search of a telephone box that hadn't had the mindless attentions of the local vandals.

We were starting to struggle a bit because either they had used them as their own public convenience, leaving behind the contents of a good night out at the pub or curry house, or more commonly, as their own personal cash dispenser, thus rendering the thing totally unusable. That said, a phone box even without glass in it would have been slightly more comfortable and a damn sight less draughty than the toilet I was supposed to be using in camp.

Eventually we located a telephone box with working parts and slightly less puddles than the rest, and I duly phoned in our report. This was in fact to my wife, who had volunteered to be the communications base for the duration of our camp. She had probably only done this to make sure I spoke to her on at least a couple of occasions during the week. Knowing that I would have ignored her until I returned home from my adventures unless she had. Although it had only been a couple of days, I was missing her and it felt good to talk, if only to reassure her that her loving husband was surviving his very first cub camp. If only just!

With the report done and having taken much longer to find a working telephone than we had anticipated, Akela and I set off at break neck speed back towards camp. We hurtled along leafy lanes and muddy tracks with our rubbish-laden trailer swishing from side to side in that worrying dance normally reserved for caravans on motorways.

From Mafeking to Molehills

Braking hard, Akela brought the Volvo to a screeching halt behind a procession of "Snoblets on Naglets" as Akela liked to call them. Trotting two by two, they bobbed up and down in that bone-jarring manner they all seem to enjoy so much. Dozens of horses and riders. All wearing silly little grins with smug expressions that all young country girls seem to wear when they are blocking up the traffic. They were travelling at no more than three miles per hour, as is their right, fully aware that the vehicle behind them was probably in a hurry.

We had had to break so firmly to avoid them that we almost turned the trailer over in the process, jack-knifing out of control and managing to miss the cavalry by no more than a few inches. Thankfully no one was hurt and the up side was that we had managed to land a couple of our own smelly deposits on the road in the form of plastic bags that had fallen out of the trailer.

We continued on, a little at a loss as to what we should do with our cargo. By this time we had travelled a fair few miles and seen nothing that resembled a suitable dump site in which we could dispose of our rubbish. There seemed little point in taking it back to camp and we were getting pretty desperate to find a solution. My suggestion of lobbing it over the nearest hedge had gone down like the Titanic and I was promptly apologising and promising to swot up on the country code, when suddenly steaming towards us out of the late morning mist, like some great snorting dragon was the local corporation dustcart.

Black smoke billowed from its vertical exhausts as it charged menacingly towards us like a raging bull. It was already dropping rubbish from the fully laden back as it careered and wallowed from side to side over every bump and pothole in the road. We just couldn't believe our luck! But there it was, off on its rounds to all the honest rate paying residents of whichever county we had managed to stumble into.

As it passed, the lorry's occupants oblivious to what was about to happen next were happily smiling and waving back at Akela as she tried to flag them down. Contentment reigned; their only thoughts were of productivity bonuses for collecting their quota of rubbish in the strict allocation of union time. You know, the time before the bookies and the bars open, commonly known as the working day for most council employees. Merrily they trundled on their way, blissfully ignorant of what was coming.

Akela, never one to be deterred, and in true movie fashion, jumped back into the car, gunned the engine and with the wheels spinning and tyres squealing, set off in hot pursuit of this poor defenceless dustcart. Well, absolutely no contest whatsoever.

Anybody who has met Akela knows exactly what I mean. There we were, completely out of control, barrelling down this country lane hardly wider than a chopstick, side by side in a duel with the dustbin lorry. The poor occupants were frightened out of their minds, all too terrified to turn their heads and look into the eyes of this demented woman, struggling to understand why on earth this mad woman, who was obviously some sort of terrorist, should want to hijack a corporation dustcart.

We diced for mile upon mile in a death defying dual and once again managed to scatter the "Snoblets and Naglets" as she left all in her wake. Akela, red faced with determination and wearing an expression that was just a little scary, eventually overhauled the truck and expertly forced this enormous lorry, all ten tons of it into a tiny lay-by that had been cut neatly into the hedgerow. Jumping from the car, even before it had stopped sliding sideways to a halt, she then jogged past the front of the lorry with its engine hissing and steaming, and casually proceeded to fling the contents of the trailer into the back of the dustcart.

By this time, I had slithered deep into the foot well of the car and was trying my best to hide from the four huge blokes who were now starting to gather their composure. Growing more and more confident and realising that maybe they weren't going to get side swiped by an AK47, the bewildered occupants began to get a little braver. One poor soul, all eighteen stone of him, even plucked up enough courage to jump down from the cart and ask in no uncertain terms what the hell she thought she was doing. The reply was so caustic that he scampered back to the relative safety of the cab and the protection of his mates with the look of a scolded cub scout.

Having emptied the trailer, Akela merely shot him a final 'nasty little man look' before nonchalantly chucking the last bin bag full of camp rubbish over her shoulder and into the back of the now overflowing dustcart. As she brushed herself down she informed him sternly that she was in fact a fully paid up ratepayer of Wiltshire. She was perfectly entitled to dispose of her rubbish as and where she saw fit and that included his lorry. This said and without further ado she hopped back into the car.

Slowly looking around to see where I had got to, she adjusted her hair in the rear view mirror, turned and gave me one of those 'call yourself a man' looks, stuck her arm out of the car window and politely waved a royal goodbye. Leaving behind what can only be described as a sorry scene of four speechless and very frightened dustmen, shaking their heads at the cheek of it all and in total disbelief, no doubt praying never again to see this particular raving lunatic, dressed in a funny uniform.

When I gingerly pointed out to Akela that we were in fact deep in the heart of Dorset and not Wiltshire, and that she had probably lost them their work bonus, she just shrugged. God knows what those poor dustmen must have thought.

CHAPTER SIX

On our return to Great Yews the cubs were busy lashing long pieces of bamboo together with small lengths of string. They were attempting to make various gadgets for their kitchens. These gadgets were to keep the plastic bowls used for the washing up, along with their plates and eating utensils, off the ground. In a similar way to a draining board at home. The idea was to try and keep the eating utensils as clean and as far from the floor and sheep shit as possible. It also allowed the washing up to be done in an upright position, making the task which was never easy when kneeling on muddy ground, slightly less arduous.

The effectiveness, with which the lashings were tied, always difficult on smooth bamboo, would determine how long the gadget stood up for. I would examine the knots before taking mental bets with myself as to how long it would take before the apparatus keeled over. Falling like some wobbling drunk, legs twisting as it collapsed into a crumpled heap.

We would spend most evenings during the washing up, waiting for the basins full of soapy water to fall through the gap in the framework, as it moved and twisted in all directions under the weight of the water. When this did happen, it would send plumes of foamy geysers skywards, scattering cubs in all directions as the water returned to earth. Great for a laugh but not so good for the washing up, and most of the hot water that the cubs had managed to boil, which usually wasn't very much, was wasted on this regular fountain display.

The afternoons at camp were allocated to visiting sites of interest, and the Wednesday, which incidentally was our last full day at Great Yews, was to be spent at the Bovington tank museum.

As usual we set off in convoy and it wasn't long before we were snuggled nicely in our warm minibus heading towards Bovington.
The weather hadn't been great and because of my inexperience of camping and the complete lack of proper kit, I had only managed to grab a few hours' sleep during the entire four days and three freezing nights of cub camp.

I was starting to sag a little and I was in desperate need of a hot shower, a cuddle from my wife and a week of undisturbed sleep in my beautifully comfortable, warm, cosy, soft, scrummy, lovely, yummy bed.

The Reluctant Cub Scout

The museum was great, and lived up to all our expectations. Full of interesting things to occupy the boys whilst we, the adults all scurried off to the toilets to find much relief, and then to the cafeteria for a welcome cup of drinkable tea.

When we were out and about we were always greeted by very odd looks and strange sniffs from most of the population. They would shuffle over to the other side of whichever café or supermarket we had called into. This was done in an attempt to get as far away as possible from the strange pong that was emanating from these scruffy Herbert's with coloured neckerchiefs on. Still, it meant we didn't have to queue for much, and getting a table was always easy as most people would quickly move away or abandon whatever they were eating in a desperate bid to escape the musty smell.

Having forty or so people in a party can cause a problem for enterprises such as the tank museum. Regrettably the cubs would swamp everything, completely taking over in their enthusiasm to see and touch as much as possible. So, in an effort to let some other patrons see something of the displays, the Curator suggested that they open up the cinema that was normally closed at this time of day. They would give 10th Camberley cub pack a private and exclusive showing of a few short films of these wonderful tanks in action. Great!

We filed in gratefully, and were immediately enveloped into the peace and tranquillity offered by the small dark room. The cubs all sat in the first few rows, the adults as far away as was possible in a small cinema. We all settled down quietly to watch what was to be an interesting and action packed show.

Regrettably that's all I, and the rest of the adults can remember...... The combination of darkness, warmth, and very comfortable seats were all too much for our tired and weary bodies, and within a few minutes all had been lulled into a deep and blissful sleep.

We would have been there all night if it hadn't been for the slightly embarrassed attendant shaking us awake. He politely advised us that the films had long since finished and that we should herd up the cubs that were now scattered all over the museum causing mayhem. His wry smile told us this certainly hadn't been the first or last time a group of people smelling like kippers had fallen asleep in his cinema.

The Reluctant Cub Scout

After what seemed an age we managed to round up our wayward cubs. Most of them were in the souvenir shop spending their pocket money that had been allocated earlier in the day. With pockets full of gifts for their younger brothers and sisters, they all piled back into the mini buses for the short journey back to Great Yews. Still bubbling from the excitement of the afternoon, we were now all looking forward to the camp fire that was traditionally held on the last night of camp.

Supper was a banquet, being the last cooking the boys would be doing on open fires during this camp. Most of the surplus wood, excluding the very large logs, was thrown onto the individual cooking fires. This made the cooking a little easier than normal, and in an effort to use up as much of the excess rations as possible, Akela had offered a huge selection of things to toss into the culinary pot. This was followed by an assortment of puddings ranging from fruit salad to rice pudding and apple pies with bananas and custard and enough delights to satisfy even the appetite of Kevin Dumpling our very own resident Billy Bunter.

Robert and Mike Harrison busied themselves with the preparations for the 'campfire' that was going to be held in the hunting lodge. Akela, and myself, who by now was slowly getting the hang of it, along with a few of the other helpers, set about collecting all the kitchen and cooking equipment for checking and storing before we left the next day.

Although the five days and especially the nights had seemed long, with some mornings starting as early as five o'clock and finishing way past midnight, the time spent at Great Yews, like most good things, had passed quickly. The thought of spending only one more night beneath the stars saddened most of the adults who, like me, had found the experience so exhilaratingly different to that of our normal everyday lives.

The camp was very much an educational affair. Although uncomfortable most of the time, the rewards gained in watching the boys develop into better children whilst learning how to work as a team was, to say the least, refreshing. All the boys had made a contribution to the camp and in general had survived by having to fend very much for themselves. To me it was an invaluable and inspirational lesson, and I promised myself that if allowed, I would return for a second dose of this magnificent tonic of happy children at one with nature.

As darkness fell we all gathered into the cosy hunting lodge. We were warmed by the roaring fire and stared dreamily into the dancing flames that had been stoked awake by Robert and the last remaining logs. The burning wood spat menacingly in the grate as if warning the boys not to get too close.

Akela lovingly distributed cocoa and biscuits to the cubs as they listened to Robert explaining where scouting had begun and proceeded to tell the story of Robert Baden Powell about his times in South Africa and his duties as the commander of a fort in the town of Mafeking. Apparently he was very short of men and was being besieged by the enemy, not a good thing. Anyway, desperate to get information and messages of help to the outside world, he decided to use the young boys who were now living and sheltering from the enemy within the fort. To give these youngster half a chance and for their safety and wellbeing he taught these young boys various skills such as tracking and trailing; communication using codes and the basic survival skills required to stay alive.

 So impressed with these young men was Baden Powell that when he finally managed to get safely home to England he published a periodical, to be purchased for a few pence each week about scouting. It was so well received and so popular amongst the young men who lived locally that Lord Baden Powell as he was to become, started up the Scout movement; and from little acorns.........

Having told the story with all the enthusiasm of a good teacher Robert went on to explain what was necessary and what had to be done in the morning. With this duty done, he suggested that someone should get up and start singing something. Reluctantly at first and then with more confidence a great chorus of 'Old Macdonald Had a Farm' erupted from the boys and was promptly followed by an assortment of strange farmyard noises, with muggins here strutting around doing chicken impressions or whatever other animal was mentioned, much to everyone's amusement. It wasn't long before the rafters were humming as 10th Camberley sang their hearts out in a celebration of surviving yet another cub camp.

As the sun rose next morning, warming the campsite into life, and after yet another night of the zipper ritual, a realisation suddenly dawned on me. Being too frightened to venture far, scared by the shadows of the yew tree forest with all it ghostly shapes and noises, my attempts to relieve myself had been somewhat lazy. I had merely padded a few paces around the side of my tent just far enough away to avoid any trickle reaching my bed. I had then stood, eyes closed and peed, zipped up my fly turned and snuggled back into my tent.

Now, on closer inspection, I discovered that for whatever reason, the lettuce kept in open trays and used daily for the lunch time picnic had been stacked that night outside the store tent. Strategically placed within striking distance of a man peeing with his eyes tightly shut, whilst shivering in the dark.

I suggested to Akela that it might be a good idea if we put something else in the sandwiches that lunch time or at least get rid of the lettuce. But she merely gave me one of those questioning looks of hers and muttered something about lettuce being good for you.
"Not this lot," I mumbled under my breath and went off to spend a frantic thirty minutes flushing every limp leaf through freezing cold water in a desperate bid to get rid of the evidence. Needless to say I skipped lunch, much to everyone's surprise. I was usually the first in the queue and this particular lunch was to be the last food we would have until we got back home to Camberley.

Striking camp is probably the worst thing in the world. Not only because nobody wants to go home but also because after five hard days, we were completely done in. We had to pack away in a few short hours what had been unpacked and put up over the duration of the camp. The task was very nearly impossible, especially in the time allotted before the 'man with a van' turned up to cart it all away.

A mad flurry would ensue before we checked the field for the last time. All of us lined up in what looked like a police search party, as we spread out in a human chain collecting the final pieces of paper, rubbish and the odd reluctant tent peg.

After making sure nothing or, more importantly no one, had been left behind we said our farewells to our trusty campsite and headed back to civilisation. Or whatever we call this madness in which we live.

CHAPTER SEVEN

Lyndhurst School was originally founded in 1895 and moved to its present site as a proprietary school in 1958, teaching girls and boys from the ages of four to eleven. Although the school would be classified as small by most standards, with fewer amenities than most of its larger neighbours, Robert and Akela, who moved to Lyndhurst in 1985 certainly made the most of what they had.

Receiving the respect they undoubtedly deserved from children and parents alike, it was their devotion and care towards the pupils who were lucky enough to attend, that made Lyndhurst a very special place indeed. It was for these reasons that Carolyn and I chose to send our own children, James and Victoria to the school.

Shortly after arriving at Lyndhurst, Akela formed the 10th Camberley Cub Scout pack as an extra curriculum activity. Most boys attending the school who are eligible to join cubs attend 10th Camberley. This makes the pack a very popular group indeed, being patronised by up to 40 boys at any one time. The advantage of being a school pack is that the boys know each other very well, and of course Akela knows them even better.

From Mafeking to Molehills

Very little got past Akela. Anybody trying it on, misbehaving or pushing their luck was brought into line very quickly. On some occasions this has caused friction between Akela and the parents but generally the pack is a very happy one, meeting every Thursday at 4 o'clock in the school hall.

Someone once said 'Show me the boy at seven and I will show you the man.' Probably true, but in my case it's 'Show me the boy at seven and I will also show you a boy at thirty-five thoroughly enjoying himself, playing at being a Cub Scout helper.' Doing all the things I hadn't managed as a child. Building camps, making fires, tracking and trailing, compass reading, playing hide and seek, forming raiding parties, making gadgets, night hiking, learning camp crafts and generally behaving in a way that if it hadn't been disguised behind the title of 'uniformed helper', would have been deemed a little odd.

It's not often you are given the opportunity to recapture some of your childhood and Thursdays have become very special to me. Long after my own son had left Lyndhurst and the cubs, which is normally the time other parents would stop helping, I was there running around like a lunatic getting strange looks from the boys who even now, probably don't know what to expect or make of me.

In the summer months cubs would be held outside and provided the weather was good enough it would allow us to venture out to the great wide world. This was usually either the local army ground at Barossa or, on very rare occasions, we were fortunate enough to be able to use the Royal Military Academy at Sandhurst itself.

It was on one such occasion that we had excitedly left Lyndhurst after the compulsory roll call and marched, or should I say ambled, down to the RMA. We were probably a little short on helpers and I will use this as an excuse for the events that followed. To this day I still shudder to think of what might have been!

We had been rummaging around the RMA for a while and as we were in the army grounds, decided to play hide and seek. You now the sort of thing, pretending to be soldiers looking for the enemy. All very realistic and that, some going off to hide in the woods and shrubbery whilst the others searched.

As always when we were enjoying ourselves so much, time had pushed on. Realising we were late as usual, Akela whistled everybody in and after quickly collecting our belongings, we hurried off to start the half mile walk to Lyndhurst and home.

To others, it seemed every time we went out with the cubs we were late getting back and a few of the parents were getting a little miffed. Like most of us with busy schedules they had other things to do. It was never done intentionally. Trying to drag thirty cubs away from what was great fun always proved difficult and this time was to be no exception.

We walked briskly back to school still high and happy from our adventures. We had made it back to the rear gate of the school in double quick time, congratulating ourselves on yet another successful cub pack meeting, when suddenly one of the boys came up to me and asked where Nicholas Wade was.

"Who's Nicholas Wade?" I replied, still not that familiar with all the boys' names.

"You Know, Nicholas" he whined, seemingly exasperated that I didn't remember his very best friend.

"Er I don't think he was with us" I said trying to convince myself.

"Yes he was Mr Laidlaw," said the little chap who by then had started to look worried.

The Reluctant Cub Scout

Calling ahead to Akela who was always able to walk at a pace that even Linford Christie would have had trouble keeping up with, I explained that somebody called 'Wade' wasn't here and could she remember whether or not he had been with us.

As the colour drained from Akela's face it suddenly dawned on us that we hadn't taken a roll call before leaving the RMA. Probably a court martial offence in the cubs.... Panic!
"Oh my God. We must have left him behind!" she yelled.
"We'll have to go back and find him, and quickly" she said as she buried her face in her hands.

That's easier said than done in hundreds of acres of army ground, I thought.
We explained red faced to Robert, who had been waiting impatiently by the back gate in readiness to deliver the customary ear bashing for being late back, that we had managed to lose one of his prized pupils. Thus dumping most of the responsibility into his lap.
"I'll call the Academy and tell them you're on your way back" he said. "Maybe they can help".

Well, help was a bit of an understatement. By the time Robert, Akela along with a couple of worried parents and myself arrived at the gate of the RMA; most of the officers destined for the British army were waiting for us. This included a dozen Ghurkhas who had been out on manoeuvres, already to look for young Nicholas Wade!

It's at times like these that you start to realise the responsibility that comes with certain jobs. Here we were searching for a child who had been left in the care of the school, the light was beginning to fade and the situation, quite frankly, was getting pretty serious.

For Robert, his job as Headmaster and therefore his responsibility for the welfare and well being of every child in his school was, at that point in time, not very appealing. I was imagining the tabloid headlines "IDIOT AND AKELA LOSE CUB SCOUT"..... "BOY LEFT IN WOODS, ABANDONED BY USELESS ASSISTANT".

Hoping and praying that perhaps Nicholas had just gone home, Akela, with me as support, drove around to his house. Firstly, we wanted to see if he was there and secondly, of course, to tell his worried parents what had happened.

We wanted to reassure them that everything that could be done was being done, and that everything would be all right. We stood on the doorstep and explained briefly what had happened and waited for the deserved tirade. Well, either they didn't understand the implications of what we were saying, or they had such faith in the school that they just didn't care.

"Oh don't worry about Nicholas" said Mr Wade. "He often does this sort of thing. I'm sure he'll be home before long," and with that he turned his back and walked towards the kitchen to continued with whatever he had been doing. Akela and I just looked at each other in astonishment and disbelief, shrugged our shoulders and went back to continue the desperate search for their precious son.

"You go right," pointing along the path towards the woods, "and I'll go left around by the lake" I said. "Just keep blowing the whistle, he's bound to hear it, and don't worry. I'm sure we'll find him," I said trying to comfort myself.

I was still imagining the front page headlines of the tabloids and wondered whether I could ever live with myself if anything bad had happened to Nicholas. I was just in the last throes of bargaining with God, when, as if by some miracle, Nicholas appeared from the southernmost part of the lake.

From Mafeking to Molehills

He was hand in hand with a middle-aged woman who was walking briskly towards us. She had found him apparently abandoned, lost and crying, while she was out walking her dog.

"Where on earth have you been?" I shouted just a little too sternly. "Didn't you hear the whistle when we finished the game?" I said. "Why did you run off?"

"No wonder he ran away if you speak to all your cubs like that," said the woman still acting as guardian to this little lost boy. But she could see the obvious relief on my face and reluctantly handed her charge over, patting him gently on the head, as she said her goodbyes.

"Thank you," I called as we walked back to the relief and cheers from all quarters as Nicholas and I hurriedly returned to the pre-arranged rendezvous.

After some gentle interrogation it turned out that Nicholas, bless him, had never played the game of hide and seek before. He thought that because we started the game by blowing a whistle, the more we blew, the deeper into the woods he had to go. By the time he realised the game had finished and that everyone else had gone home, he was completely and utterly lost! Can you imagine this terrified child, deep in the middle of thick woodland with the night and all its horrors quickly closing in? Alone and completely lost. Pretty scary stuff even for a fully-grown adult, let alone an eight-year-old boy who only wanted to be a Cub Scout. He is probably still having nightmares poor little soul. I know I would be.

Thankfully no real harm was done and as they say, all's well that ends well. If nothing else, we now make sure we take several roll calls whenever we go anywhere.

CHAPTER EIGHT

Akela very much enjoyed running the cub pack and spent most of her time devising games, projects and events so that the boys who eagerly attended would find the time interesting. They avidly collected badges that would stretch half way down their arms.

There were badges for tracking and trailing, home help, sports and hobbies. Virtually every subject you can think of was covered, except silently farting on parade, for which most of them would have collected several armfuls. However, badges were not given out lightly and the cubs would very much have to earn them.

Thankfully this gave me the opportunity to help in some small way, assisting them in their various challenges. In most cases I would have to teach myself things from the Baden Powell books 'Scouting for Boys' just a few seconds before trying to explain to the eager to learn cubs the likes of compass bearing or complicated knots called 'sheep shanks'.

On many occasions I would trip myself up and have to bluster my way out of a chasm when some smart arse of a ten-year-old, fresh from the classroom would easily prove me wrong. 'Who's teaching who?' I would often think to myself, knowing the answer to that question already. It was the feedback from the cubs that opened my eyes and heart in the first place. I soon gained an understanding of why people choose to become teachers. Although if I were a teacher, and thankfully I'm not, most of any class left in my care for any more than a couple of hours, would undoubtedly have been in chaos, with most of the pupils strangled by the end of the lesson.

There were a couple of things I managed to learn whilst in the Church Lads Brigade. The first one was how to blow a bugle whilst braking wind in harmony, not very hard when you are blowing with all your might into something that doesn't want to make a noise, only to get a strange farty noise out of both ends when you did succeed. The other was, wait for it, semaphore signalling. Yes, I know a life skill for every day use.

For the less informed, one is a method of sending a signal by means of moving wind, the other by moving flags. Where the hell you find a bugle or a pair of flags whilst stuck up a hill, or deep in danger, God only knows.

I can honestly say that in my fifty odd years of life I have never once had to draw on this fantastic knowledge, or even come close to using the art of semaphore to save myself. Still there's plenty of time yet, let's just hope the good Samaritan who comes to my rescue was also a member of the C.L.B or some other organisation that taught the skill of reading the communication technique of mad flag waving.

As this was one of the badges under the section of Signs and Signalling that the cubs could achieve, and after bragging proudly to Akela that I knew how to do it, we decided to traipse along with the cubs to the Ministry of Defence land at Barossa, climb up 'Badger Hill', named for obvious reasons, and practise the skill of semaphore.

The day itself wasn't very bright and this matched my mood exactly. Accompanied by a cold northerly wind that nipped and stung as it blew bitterly round our ears at every opportunity, we marched off in an over-excited shambles towards Barossa and 'Badger Hill'.

In our enthusiasm we hadn't noticed that the higher we climbed the more exposed to the elements we were getting, until that is, it was all too late. We assembled at the top of the hill in a tight circle trying to protect ourselves as much as possible from the howling gale that was buffeting the boys' backs and proceeded to make our flags. These were constructed 'Heath

The Reluctant Cub Scout

Robinson' style from bits of coloured paper and sticky tape, attached as best as possible, around a couple of thin bamboo sticks.

Then came the eye poking bit, followed by the inevitable sword fighting, followed by me screaming at the top of my voice trying to make myself heard over the howling wind. Eventually with lots of jostling we managed to get the cubs assembled into some sort of order, far enough apart so they didn't cause themselves or each other too much damage each time they stuck their flags out.

I faced the boys and started with some basic movements, how to stand with flags crossed A, B, C. and so on. But it wasn't very long before it dawned on me that by facing them, I was in fact teaching them backwards. Everything they did was in mirror image. So turning around to face nobody but the badgers I started all over again.

Picture the scene, muggins here out in front, with thirty cubs behind, perched on top of a very large hill, wind howling, madly flapping our arms about in what must have looked to anybody who was passing like a poor attempt at flying.

From Mafeking to Molehills

I was soon bored with practice and the embarrassment of constantly contradicting myself because my brain had frozen from the continuous battering it was receiving from the icy gales. Couple this with the fact that, as with all eight, nine and ten year olds, the boys were ever eager and even more impatient to try their newly acquired skills. So I gave up and decided to split the pack into two groups. One on either side of the hill in an attempt to see if it were possible to send a readable message to each other...... Fat chance.

A young lad called Morgan, with the very apt surname of Bird, was prancing about flapping his flags up and down like the wings of some giant albatross. I suggested that he should 'stop messing about' and that he face the group I was with and start sending a message we could all read. "Something simple!" I shouted.
"Like Morgan," someone yelled to a chorus of laughter.
"All right Mr Laidlaw," he mouthed, as by now any attempt at speech was uselessly whisked away and lost forever in the wind that was now blowing full into the little lad's face.

Morgan, honoured at being selected, and for once doing what he was told, stood facing the group of perished cubs who were still huddled together as closely as possible in a desperate attempt to hide from the elements and patiently waited for Morgan to start his signal.

P, everybody shouted in harmony, L, came the roar, E, the same chorus and so on, until we had managed with an awful lot of guessing to spell out the first word of his message, PLEASE. I was really impressed. Pleased he was doing so well, and chuffed to bits that the cubs could actually read it. Then came the second word, G, I, T. Umm, not so good, still, plod on. Then the third, fourth, fifth until he had spelt out letter by letter his desperate message or should I say plea, which read. "Please git me off this hill, I'm freezing."

With that subtle hint and with tears running down my cheeks, partly from laughter but mostly from the wind, I suggested we pack up and go home. No sooner said than they all cheered and stampeded headlong down the side of 'Badger Hill'. Everybody flapping their flags, squawking "I'm a Barosa bird, I'm a Barosa bird, look Mr Laidlaw, I'm a Barosa bird." I smiled as Akela and I slowly ambled down the hill too cold to move very fast and much too numb to shout for them to stop. For once we just allowed them to run wild down the hill, if for no other reason than to get them warm.

CHAPTER NINE

As the pack grew in numbers additional helpers were drafted in, willing parents like myself who wanted to give back to the school and subsequently the cubs, something in return for the enjoyment gained by their children.

One such volunteer was an American called Tom Feely. Tom, who was currently living in England and working as a flight attendant for one of the American airlines, was married to Ulla, a very attractive six foot blond from Sweden. Both were lovely people and had two fine boys who attended Lyndhurst School.

Tom and I enjoyed each other's company, and would quite often play golf together. However, as you would expect, a lot of our time was taken up with the inevitable friendly banter. The 'them' and 'us' syndrome. You know, how the Yanks won the war for us. How they always kicked our butts at everything sporty. How funny we talked, and how quaint we were for sticking our little fingers out when we drank tea after a soccer or cricket match. Most of it light hearted and sometimes amusing.

Tom was into martial arts, with a burning ambition to be a black belt in Tai kwon-do by the time he reached forty. With this goal in mind he would spend every waking hour stretching and moving in a majestic way that most schoolgirls attending ballet class on Saturday mornings would have died for.

Forever practising, his limbs would flash out in all directions without warning, followed by grunting or whooshing noises as he expelled all the energy from his mind, body or wherever part necessary, in a perfect act of power and self control. You had to truly admire the dedication and determination of the man, but like all things, there is a time and place for everything.

Tom, by this stage of his training, was unable to stand still for more than a couple of seconds. He had a constant need to move for fear of stiffening up. Whilst on parade one Thursday, with all the cubs standing neatly to attention, saluting the flag, Akela proudly looking on, he suddenly stuck a leg out, a well measured kick placed right under Akela's nose, missing her by millimetres as he attempted to stretch as much as possible, seemingly oblivious to what was going on around him. Then he slowly retracted the limb from its obscure angle, and carried on as if nothing had happened.

From Mafeking to Molehills

Although an unbelievable feat of suppleness, this manoeuvre really pissed Akela off. So much so that in return, she flashed him such a stern and withering look, so deadly in its stare that it scared our resident black belt to death. Akela, all nine stone of her had been capable of striking with one small glance, far more fear into him than any ring hardened street fighter was ever likely to do.

On one particular and, it must be said, typical Thursday, Tom and I were asked to take the fifth and sixth form cubs to the Military Museum at Aldershot. So with the help of Cathy Boundy, another willing parent, we set off with about fifteen boys to explore the mysteries and horrors of the weaponry used in the past great wars.

Like most of Akela's excursions the preparation and planning was excellent. Regrettably the execution was as always something different and this Thursday was to be no exception. On our arrival at the museum, no one was expecting us.
"We haven't got the manpower to look after you today," explained an over starched and overdressed officer. "Some sort of communications cock up old chap. Sorry and all that but you will have to call back some other day," he proclaimed, and promptly turned

around and marched smartly back towards the barracks. Having travelled the ten miles to Aldershot we were determined not to be fobbed off and chased after the officer in an effort to change his mind.

In reality it didn't take much persuasion as the boys all performed their big puppy dog eyes bit along with a practised 'butter wouldn't melt in my mouth' routine. This coupled with firm assurances from me, and a guarantee that every thing would be tickerty boo we managed to convince this poor unsuspecting officer that the adults present were quite capable of looking after a few little boys who would dearly love to see all the rare and priceless memorabilia from a bygone age. Boys who would truly benefit from the wealth of educational stimulation offered by his fine museum and no we wouldn't touch anything, promise! promise! promise!

Well what happened next probably shortened the careers of at least two British fighting men and probably the officer as well. Fine upstanding men. Men who had, until then, never met their match. Men who had trained hard, to think on their feet, to react with lightning speed to any given situation. To face adversity and show no fear and, sadly, men who, regardless of how much training they'd been given, stood absolutely no chance against fifteen 10th Camberley cubs scouts.

From the minute the smirking youngsters walked past the two soldiers on duty, and into the museum, we lost control. The boys scattered in all directions, leaping on machine guns, popping into tank turrets, climbing onto motor bikes, into anything and everything they could get their hands on. Anything they weren't meant to touch, they touched. It was complete pandemonium. Not really the boys' fault, they were just a little over enthusiastic. After all, playing war games is part of any boy's childhood and this lot was no exception. They were pulling levers, rat-a-tat-tatting all over the place, shouting, screaming, making bomb noises and generally having a great time.

Then suddenly came the silence, a hushed quiet that you could almost touch. You know the sort of silent hush you get when someone has managed to do something exceptionally bad and I mean really, really bad, even for ten year olds.
"Mr Laidlaw!" came the dreaded cry and from a section of the museum dedicated to 'Rare guns from the Second World War' I witnessed a couple of cubs sneaking away from the scene of the crime on tiptoe, guilt written all over their faces.

The Reluctant Cub Scout

The scene that lay before us was indescribable. Mass devastation on a scale not seen in Aldershot since the IRA bombings. Total destruction and in particular an object that had, up until then been a superb looking machine gun. This magnificent piece of engineering had proudly stood the test of time and had been singled out and positioned in the centre of the display. Surviving its retirement for over forty years unscathed and untouched. It now lay in pieces with its entire contents of working parts spewed out all over the oil stained floor, its main spring dangling like some headless jack-in-the-box with gun oil dripping in puddles around the debris, and not a cub in sight.

The audible cry from the two army guys on duty could be heard from across the museum and the look of complete horror etched on each of their faces was enough to tell me that something monumental had happened. Unable to come to terms with what they were witnessing or believe that a few eight, nine, and ten-year-old boys had managed to achieve, in less than twenty minutes, what the Boer and two world wars had failed to do, very nearly made these poor chaps pass out. Ashen faced, they explained that it was their solemn and only duty to ensure that nothing untoward happened to the contents of the museum whilst they were on guard duty.

"Christ, what have they done?" sobbed the young corporal as the realisation sank in. "You had better go" he said while wringing the beret in his hands in an action that very much made its point.

"No one is going to believe this," sighed the other soldier as he slowly shook his head from side to side in disbelief and in the certain knowledge that his career in the army had, without doubt, just ended. Tearful in the sad acceptance of inevitability, he started muttering something about a court-martial and firing squads as he quickly ushered us out of what I must say had been a very fine museum.

After stuttering my apologies for the umpteenth time we stumbled out of the building and across the gravel car park. We tried to herd the sheepish boys back to the cars as quickly as possible whilst hoping and praying that the ground would open up and swallow us all. Not once did we dare glance back as we promptly left Aldershot and the two forlorn soldiers standing in the doorway of the Aldershot Military Museum for fear of seeing grown men in army uniform bawling their eyes out. Numb from the experience, Tom, Cathy and myself spent the rest of the journey back to Camberley racking our brains for a plausible excuse to give to Akela. Not about the damage to the museum you understand, we had already made a pact never to tell Akela, but why we were home twenty minutes early.

CHAPTER TEN

Under the division of Surrey Heath, the cubs would be invited to attend most of the activities organised by the county. This would include team events such as five-a-side football, night hiking and a swimming gala normally held late in the year. Akela would ask the boys to volunteer to attend these events and would get buried by requests from the eager cubs wishing to be included in the teams. So in an effort not to disappoint too many of the younger ones, Akela would stick four teams into the football competition and at least two teams into the swimming gala.

The five-a-side football was played at the leisure centre at Woking and was always a popular and very well attended day. It gave the opportunity for the bigger or more talented cubs to show off their skills. The seeding of the groups was such that most of the "A" and "B" teams would progress through a league system to the final stages.

The finals were played in a sudden death knockout format and would cause fearsome competition between the various cub leaders who took these events a little too seriously. They would scream at the poor guy who had volunteered to referee that they were cheating or were biased against their pack whenever they lost or a dodgy decision was given against them. This of course, was not the case and it must be said that generally the best team won on the day with matches always being played with good-natured rivalry amongst the cubs themselves.

10th Camberley never let themselves down. It was always a little difficult to watch our C and D teams, like the Christians of old being thrown amidst the lions and tigers only to be slaughtered five or six goals to nil, by the more experienced players. Flinching as balls whistled past their ears from a 'David Beckham' type volley, I would watch our little goal keeper who was knee high to a pot plant getting back ache from picking the ball out of the goal net so many times. Still, as they say, it was good character building stuff and they would eagerly put up their hands the next time, a little older and slightly wiser, desperate to eradicate last year's nightmares and hopefully to gain revenge.

The Swimming Gala was something else. To this day I still don't understand why year after year 10th Camberley managed to crush all in their wake, wiping the floor with all who opposed. They don't have a pool at Lyndhurst school, nor do we practise prior to the event.

The boys were the same size as all the other teams but every year the same thing happened. We would stand, slightly embarrassed at the end of the event, collecting virtually every prize on offer, with the exception of 'the life jacket relay!'....

The 'Splasharama' as it was officially named would be split into two main sections, proper grown up swimming, breast stroke and so forth and then, to keep the not-so-capable swimmers happy, various fun relay races. These activity races would be swum widthways across the pool and involve swapping balls, balloons and err...life jackets.

Akela, as was her wont, and knowing how much I enjoyed running the teams, would plonk me in charge for the night. Still not being fully acquainted with all the boys or their names, I would guess who was who and put them on the team sheets. In some cases I would get it wrong and be corrected by the boys themselves as to who could swim and who would quite simply drown, but all in all I usually managed to get away with it.

Over the years, hundreds of cubs drift through the pack, starting at eight and in the case of 10th Camberley, leaving at the age of eleven. All individuals in their own right, some fat, some thin, some tall and some small ones, long ones and short ones, some bright, some very bright and even, for the want of being kind, the not so bright, and then there was... Kevin Dumpling!

Kevin was the first fat vegetarian I think I have ever met. Genetically large, as both his parents were also huge, poor Kevin would waddle about under the handicap of being at least three stone heavier than the rest of the world. Most of the other cub members were like stick insects and Kevin would regrettably, but understandably, be the butt of a lot of the school jokes. He was a likeable fellow and would rarely be put off by the mickey taking, and so, to his credit, would enter into most things organised by the cubs, and the swimming gala was to be no exception.

Having had to go to work on the Saturday of the gala I arrived at the complex a little later than planned. I hurried into the changing rooms to organise the boys, having paid little attention to the team sheets that had been thrust at me upon my arrival, other than to make sure all the cubs were present and correct. I rushed out to the pool area just in time to hear the crackle of the loud speaker as it announced the first event.

From Mafeking to Molehills

"Right David you're number one, Kevin you're number two, Charles you're three, and Paul you're anchor," I said, pleased with my terminology and thinking to myself that at least it sounded good to anybody who might be listening.

The idea of the race was to swim the width of the pool, whilst wearing a life jacket, get out with the help of your team mate, unzip the life jacket and give it to him. That team mate would then put it on and dive back into the water and swim to the other side and so on in relay fashion. So...

"On your marks... Get set ...Bang!!"

"Great start David" I shouted over the cheering crowd of excited parents who were all willing their little boys on.

"Good keep going. That's it, faster, go on!" I screamed.

"Good, pull him out," I yelled as I watched Kevin and Paul struggle a little to heave their sodden team mate out of the pool. I noted that the now wet life jacket gushed water from its torn seams like a leaky bucket. But with great dexterity and lots of adrenaline pumping through their little veins they managed to land their catch. They expertly unzipped and slipped the life jacket onto Kevin Dumpling and after a few adjustments to the straps and a lot of wriggling from his excited team mates, we all watched Kevin launch himself into the water like some beached whale returning to the sea.

It was at this point that my credibility as team manager fell apart. Looking to the other end of the pool it suddenly dawned on me that not only had I left only one boy to haul Kevin out of the water but had managed to select Charles, who was quite easily the smallest cub in our pack. Splosh, splosh, splosh crawled Kevin relentlessly plodding along like a turtle in the bright red oversized life jacket that was now billowing out in all directions with trapped air. Eager to reach the side of the pool so as not to let his team mates down, he stretched his chubby hand out to Charles for the expected assistance and waited to be pulled out, according to the plan.

Trying to avoid the black looks that were not only coming from the Dumpling family but also Charles's parents, I started to encourage the boy to keep pulling, an impossible task even with a block and tackle let alone a single cub scout weighing less than a wet tea bag! Still, ten out of ten for trying. Charles, purple in face, with gritted teeth and both hands firmly clasped around Dumpling's plump arm was pulling with all his might, whilst Kevin with his legs flapping like a duck was trying to assist Charles in his landing.

From Mafeking to Molehills

By this time the ripples of compressed giggling had turned into wave upon wave of hysterical laughter as more and more parents spotted poor Charles tugging away at the floundering red turtle. Time after time the poor boy slid back into the water causing waves of tidal water to swamp everybody at the pool side before continuing towards the feet of the judges, who simultaneously hopped backwards in an attempt to find dry land.

Unable to assist poor Charles for fear of getting disqualified, the rest of the team could only stand and watch exasperated in the disbelief of how Mr Laidlaw could have got it all so horribly wrong. By now the race had long since finished with most of the competitors already rubbing themselves dry, and congratulating themselves on their efforts. They were all beginning to wonder why the onlookers were falling about laughing, and holding their bellies with tears rolling down their faces, only to join in after seeing Charles, red faced, still tugging as hard as he could and getting absolutely nowhere.

To save any further embarrassment to Kevin, and myself for that matter, and for fear that Charles would cause himself a little more than just permanent mental damage, I went off and found a convenient boat hook or whatever they are called. I hooked it under the neck of the life jacket and with the help of a handful of parents all struggling with the weight, we managed to haul a very damp and sodden looking Kevin from the water and land him safely on the side of the pool. There was rapturous applause from the crowd who by now had accepted that it was not the winning, but the taking part that mattered. Try telling that to Kevin!

CHAPTER ELEVEN

Keeping a gaggle of cubs scouts occupied for more than a few minutes is never very easy, especially towards the end of term. The boys have the concentration levels of goldfish. Thankfully Akela was an expert at finding new and challenging things to do. Always managing to come up with the most wondrous and ingenious projects for the boys to tackle. We would have a whale of a time stringing things together such as catapults made from bamboo canes lashed together tripod style with elastic bands. Then hold competitions as to who could fire golf balls the farthest from plastic cups that had been attached to the middle of the apparatus.The winner was generally the one who managed to bounce the golf ball of the back of my head as I ran for cover.

On other occasions we would try boiling water in home made pots made from silver foil that we hung over open fires. Only to watch the flames being slowly extinguished from the constant dribble of water that leaked from the flimsy vessels. Sometimes we would set light to rolled up pieces of corrugated cardboard that we had filled with melted candle wax. Then we would attempt to cook, or should I say cremate, a sausage as it balanced perilously on a piece of silver foil that had been hastily wrapped around an old wire coat hanger bent into the shape of a tennis racquet. It's strange that most every time I left cubs on a Thursday night during the summer it was either with a tummy ache from the uncooked offerings the boys would force me to eat or a lump on my head from the odd stray missile.

Akela had read or seen somewhere in one of her many scouting books an idea for making kites. All that was needed apparently were two small canes and a black bin liner. The idea was to cut the bin liner into a certain shape, place the canes in a cross like fashion, stick it all together with sticky tape and Bob's Your Uncle.

So one Thursday was spent in the manufacturing of these so-called kites. Thirty in all were made and I must admit I was a bit dubious as I watched the steady stream of crucified bin bags emerge from the end of the production table.

As a child, youth and adult, I had never yet managed to get a proper, top of the range kite with all the dangly bits off the ground. James, Victoria and I spent many a wasted hour running up and down Windsor Great Park scaring the deer in an attempt to flight a kite, let alone launch a bin bag. However the end product was neatly stored away, ready for our planned trip to the fields the following Thursday.

As Lyndhurst has no playing field of its own, we were going to utilise the public park area nearby. Provided you learnt how to step over the dog muck and hypodermic needles, the wide open spaces were perfect for our needs. Thursday, kite flying day arrived and True to form the British weather let us down. Not as you would expect with rain, sleet or hail, but nothing, not a puff of wind, not even a breeze blowing gently through the trees. Zilch, Nada. The day was completely still and certainly the calmest day we had had all year, and we were now well into July.

Now anybody who understands the science of kite flying and even those of us that don't know, know that you need two basic elements to master this particular skill. One is a kite, home made or otherwise, the other is wind! We only had the kite.

Akela, never one to be put off, announced to the boys that they would have to make their own wind.... Well, you get what you deserve when you ask thirty ten year olds with minds like sewers to perform a task like that. After five minutes of uncontrolled laughter we managed to explain that what Akela had meant was that they would have to run up and down the playing field in an effort to raise the kites into the air.

It gets worse. There we were watching cubs akin to headless chickens running around the field. None of them paying any attention to where they were going, bumping into everybody and anybody as they concentrated on what their precious kite was doing behind them. Some of the boys who enthusiastically criss-crossed the park would bob and weave boxing fashion, in an effort to avoid garrotting themselves on the trails of string that hung from the sky. The kites, however were slightly less enthusiastic and would spin uncontrollably as they spiralled headlong into the ground, terminally crumpling on impact before being trampled on by a stampeding cub as he rushed passed desperately trying to launch his own bin bag.

All this was happening to a chorus of encouragement and loud shouts of "Have you got it up yet?" and "Come on boys, faster, Get it up, that's better" and Go on, get it up, oh yes up it goes" from Akela.

God only knows what the local residents thought and I spotted at least three people emerge from their front doors only to return disappointed because they had failed to witnessing some rampant women chasing little boys around the local park.

Resigned to failure we abandoned the kite flying until a more favourable day and promised the disappointed boys that it wouldn't be long before we would return to conquer the skies. Now windless, not only in weather, but from the exertion of it all led us to the problem of what to do next and how to keep the cubs amused for the rest of the pack meeting.

The motto of the scouts is 'Be Prepared' and Akela was always that! Like some magician plying her trade, she produced from her trusty rope bag various pieces of string, a bundle of tent pegs, compasses and several sheets of paper.

"This might be a bit difficult to explain," she said, "so please pay attention." The idea was to start from one point, put a tent peg into the ground, tie one end of the string to the peg, take a compass reading, walk a number of paces as instructed, stop, put another peg into the ground, wrap the string around this peg and repeat. Now, provided you followed the instructions to the letter, when you had finished, you should have magically marked out and drawn with the aid of the string, a picture of an animal.

Each 'six' was given their instruction sheet, pegs and string and told to find a space large enough to set out their task. This meant that the pack was spread across the entire field, just a little too far for us to supervise continuously. After checking that one group understood what was to be done, we moved on to another. By the time we got round to the last group at the far end of the field, the first groups 'sixer' came running towards us excitedly calling that they had finished.

I must admit that I was just a little surprised, thinking it should have taken slightly longer than it had to mark, take a compass bearing, pace and mark again, but these children never cease to amaze me. So giving them the benefit of the doubt I hurried back to where they were all proudly standing in a line. Misinterpreting my grinning face as pride as I stared along this perfectly straight length of string, punctuated by the occasional tent peg.

Compass reading at the best of times, isn't that easy, and trying to grasp the concept at the ripe old age of ten is nigh on impossible. Although as instructed, they had correctly set the compass to the bearing marker each time, instead of walking in the direction of the bearing arrow clearly marked on the compass, they had waited for the needle to settle onto north as it always would and promptly followed that.

"What's that meant to be" I laughed, unable to hide my amusement any longer.

"It's obvious" they all chorused, a little bewildered at how stupid Mr Laidlaw, an adult, could be sometimes.

"Der! It's a snake Mr Laidlaw" explained the 'sixer' as they celebrated being the first group to finish the task

"Of course it its" I chuckled not having the heart to tell them anything different and walked off so that they couldn't see the tears of laughter rolling down my cheeks.

I love being a cub!

CHAPTER TWELVE

Akela was blessed with more relatives than a lottery winner and this, at times, proved to be very useful. She had, once again, called in a marker and managed to get an agreement from her cousin who was tenant farming at that time, to allow us to camp on one of the fields owned by his landlord, Lord Margadale.

Ashley Wood farm was situated on the outskirts of the pleasant village of Tisbury, a rural settlement nestling snugly within the beautiful countryside of Wiltshire. Tisbury, blessed with its compulsory pubs, post office and corner shops would probably have gone unnoticed were it not for the fact that the village boasts a mainline railway station, with direct links to the capital.

The farm was much the same as any small farm struggling to survive in the late twentieth century. It consisted mainly of ramshackle buildings roofed with rusty pieces of corrugated iron, forming makeshift shelters that rattled and banged as they flapped dejectedly in the wind.

These derelict buildings were accompanied by odd pieces of obsolete farm machinery, all scattered like hideous sculptures that lay abandon around the unkempt yards of this once thriving farm, haphazardly placed between the weeds and long grass that grew unchecked and unnoticed. Sadly it gave the general appearance of neglect and dereliction from not only the lack of investment it so badly needed, but from the lack of time and effort necessary to profitably run a modern farm.

Nothing ever seemed to go on around Ashley Wood Farm and I can honestly say that in the years we camped at Tisbury, rarely did we see anything or anybody working. Occasionally the odd gamekeeper would amble past, gun safely broken under his arm, whilst walking his dogs, but other than that, no one. Not unless of course you count the many flocks of sheep occupied in that strange production line of eating grass and making shit.
Nevertheless, we were, as always, very grateful for the use of a field, and more importantly the water tap that was attached to one of the derelict outbuildings adjacent to the farm.

The farm itself is located within the grounds of the very impressive Margadale estate, and is situated on the banks of a magnificent lake filled with deep turquoise waters coloured by the minerals it absorbs from the surrounding land. It stretches for more than a mile in length, and nearly three hundred meters wide and runs from east to west along a small valley peppered by a variety of well-established copses.

On bright sunny days, especially towards the end of May and the beginning of June the water would form a shimmering mirror from the cloudless skies, reflecting in perfect symmetry the contrasts of the fertile land. A tapestry of summer colours in multitudes of greens and bright yellows all painted on the landscape of surrounding countryside by these ever-invisible farmers.

The impressive estate house sat imposingly on the north bank of the lake and was protected from view by a line of trees that ran along the entire length of its shore line. Offering privacy and protection not only for its wealthy owners who enjoyed the solitude but also to the variety of animals that inhabited the area and who lived freely amongst its weedy banks and shady hollows. All manner of mysterious wildlife that although rarely seen during the day kept the boys awake most nights with strange blood curdling cries that would echoe across the dark and misty water.

The lake boasted its own waterfall, which acted as an overflow when rain was abundant. This would form a magical staircase of cascading water that flowed relentlessly down into crystal pools, stimulating swirling eddies that would spin off and chase each other in a spiral dance downstream. Just the right combination for cubs and pooh sticks.

On warm lazy days the boys would spend ages lashing twigs and sticks together in an effort to see who could build the finest boat. All sorts of strange craft would appear, from triangular tri- marans to things that looked like spaceships. Some were made from discarded pop bottles, others would be built with bits of paper formed into sails, some top heavy, some too heavy, and some, that sadly, had little chance of floating at all. But they were all built with loving care and were proudly paraded around before being cast, or should I say, ceremoniously lobbed, into the murky waters of the lake, to meet their fate.

Whether they were shipwrecked on the branches that protruded menacingly from the banks, like fingers pawing at its prey, or disintegrated as they hurled themselves relentlessly against the rocks at the bottom of the swirling pools, for most, the result and consequences were always tragically the same. Disaster, and always to the disbelief, dismay and utter disappointment of their builders. The boats would shatter themselves into driftwood and the debris would spin like compass needles in an endless effort to find north.

 The boys would tearfully stare into the turbulent waters in the vain hope that maybe, just maybe, their boat would have survived... After witnessing their fate, with all hands lost and all hopes dashed, they would pause for a moment as if in silent prayer, before scampering off into the woods to find bigger and better building material. Quickly returning armed with new knowledge and bundles of hope in an attempt to improve on their last unsuccessful effort.

For those lucky few that did manage to survive the perils of the deep, successfully negotiating the turbulent and choppy waters, it simply meant they floated away to a far off land. Merrily they bobbed up and down as if nodding their greeting to anyone they met. Slowly they pirouetted like dancers as they navigated gracefully past the ever-watchful gaze of the grazing sheep. Flocks upon flocks of woolly jumpers who, as they continued to feed, were blissfully unaware of the endeavours these little craft had just endured.

CHAPTER THIRTEEN

Within the grounds of the estate that surrounded the campsite were several places of interest, mostly follies and caves constructed on the whim of a previous lord. A lord with an awful lot more money than sense, or so it appeared. However, these places were ripe for the investigation and imagination of a hungry pack of inquisitive cub scouts. The cubs would spend hours climbing all over the now crumbling and derelict structures, poking and prodding to discover fossils and such like, then asking questions that I had little hope of answering knowledgeably.

Whenever they asked me a question directly, I would only respond if I was certain of the answer. If, however, as in most cases, I was unsure, I would suggest politely that they use their own brains for once and would tell them to go and find out the information for themselves.

This ruse would usually work wonders, and dug me out of many a deep hole, not to mention the fact that it kept the educational damage of these bright young buttons, to a minimum.

The Reluctant Cub Scout

All in all, Ashley Wood Farm was an ideal location, with plenty to offer in the way of amusement, with even greater activities in and around the surrounding area. This made it, for me, the most popular of all our campsites. That and the fact that Robert and Akela just happened to have purchased a lovely cottage in the village itself, easily within striking distance whenever a hot shower was needed.

We planned to arrive at Tisbury at around lunchtime on the Saturday of the May Bank Holiday weekend, leaving Camberley at about ten o'clock that morning. By now we had learnt that the easiest thing to do was to hire a 'man with a van', await his arrival and fill his van to the gunwales with the equipment. This was achieved by passing it along a chain of eager cubs.

Once completed we would send the over laden van on its way an hour or so before we were due to set off. In theory, the plan was for all of us to arrive at the campsite together, at roughly the same time. 'Together' that is until you realise the plan hadn't accounted for the fact that muggins here, famed by now for having absolutely no sense of direction at all didn't know where he was supposed to be going.

From Mafeking to Molehills

The holiday traffic was reportedly heavy on our normal route and Robert had decided to make a detour to the route that he and I had taken the previous Thursday when we had put up a couple of the tents in case of bad weather. Nor did the plan account for the fact that you cannot safely drive a minibus and successfully read a road map at the same time.

I had a couple of the parents in tow, who had been told by Akela to follow me in their cars and who were now completely reliant on 'Mr Laidlaw' to show them the way. I was reluctant to confess to anybody that I wasn't sure of where I was going, or for that matter, what I was doing. So I gingerly set off down the motorway towards Wiltshire and the camp site. It was at this point I realised that the cubs hadn't been listening to a word we'd been saying the last time we had taken them for map reading. A request for a volunteer to read the map was met with nothing but silence with the entire contents of the minibus staring blankly out of the windows.

Robert was driving the new school minibus, and along with Akela and a few of the others in their cars, set off confidently in front of us towards camp. I was driving a heap of a minibus hired from the local rental company fully laden with fifteen cub scouts and their rucksacks. I now had a top speed equivalent to that of a tortoise, and it wasn't long before my little convoy started to fall behind. Regardless of how hard I pushed the thing it was hopeless and within a few miles of being on the motorway I had managed to lose sight of the leading group.

The journey time to Tisbury was normally about an hour and a half, so after a couple of hours of blindly guessing what road to take, it dawned on me that we weren't where we were supposed to be. Unable to read the map properly and drive safely at the same time, I pulled into a lay-by, one to tell the others who were following me what was happening and two, to try and check out our location.

I staggered out of the minibus like some old drunk unable to walk properly because my legs had gone to sleep, stumbling uncontrollably into the road as I gave chase to the map that had blown from my grasp the moment I had stepped from the vehicle. This only added to my embarrassment of being lost as I walked John Wayne style around the back to where the cars that had been following me had pulled in.

I quickly explained to Cathy Boundy and Trevor James that we were lost, and hurrying for fear that the boys might touch something in the minibus they shouldn't, like the hand brake or accelerator, I promptly spread the now crumpled map over the bonnet of one of the cars. By skilfully pinning it down with the use of my arms, elbows, and knees I managed to stop it blowing away long enough to read it. After turning it around a couple of times I finally pin pointed where we were, and more importantly, where we weren't.

Dismayed to find that we were about twenty miles off course, I hurriedly refolded the map as best I could and pointed in the direction from which we had come. Whilst thinking of what excuses I could offer to Akela, something I had been doing lots of lately, I quickly checked behind me to see that all was clear and, promptly stepped out into the road. Unseen by me who was oblivious to the danger, a car was approaching us flat out whilst overtaking another vehicle and was now, not only doing over a hundred miles an hour but was now on the wrong side of the road. My feet left the ground as I found myself hurtling backwards through the air.

Thankfully not from the impact of the speeding car; but because Trevor had mercifully seen the situation and been quick-witted enough to grab the back of my coat. With an almighty tug he had yanked me backwards and skywards and fortunately out of harm's way. The car had missed me by inches and without a doubt Trevor's lightning reactions had saved my life. For several minutes afterwards we all stood there in stunned silence, under no illusion as to what had just happened and more so what might have been. Still shaking from the experience and grateful that Trevor had been volunteered for cub camp; we turned around and headed back the way we had come.

The humiliation of getting lost was compensated by the fact that by the time we got to Tisbury, nearly two hours late, most of the camp equipment had been unloaded, and the man with a van had left for home. Handy really, considering I was still suffering from my near death experience.

It later appeared that I wasn't the only one to have missed the grim reaper by inches that day, and I was intrigued to hear that Dan Bailey, who was yet another volunteered parent, had also come close to meeting his maker.

Dan had decided to nominate himself as the official camp photographer, for no other reason than to keep himself out of mischief, and had purchased a very snazzy video camera, which was all very new and exciting at the time. He had sensibly decided to follow Robert to the campsite, and was itching for an excuse to use his new toy. Apparently overwhelmed by the majestic beauty of the landscape in front of him he had picked up his camera to film the picturesque scenery whilst driving down the small country lanes leading to the farm.

Within a few moments Dan was full of creative spirit and was poetically commentating on the spectacle of fauna and flora as it travelled past his lens. Completely carried away with himself and blinkered by his viewfinder he had for a moment completely forgotten where he was and more importantly, what, in fact, he was doing.

The farm as described earlier was a little worse for wear and the fence that bordered the road, supposedly to protect the user from a sheer drop into the valley and the lake below, had long since disappeared. With nothing to indicate where the drop started or where the road ended, negotiating this track was difficult at the best of times, even with both eyes open and two hands tightly gripped on the steering wheel. To attempt to do this whilst playing David Attenborough was damn near suicidal.

The resulting footage was quite amusing. Dan went from author to composer to stunt driver and then blasphemer, in about five seconds. He had had to suddenly drop the video camera in an effort to grab the steering wheel to bring the car back under control as it failed to negotiate an extremely sharp corner. After sliding to a halt, only fractions of an inch from the edge of the ravine, he quickly decided to put his new toy away until we were firmly settled into camp. To cap it all and not surprisingly, poor Dan had forgotten to turn the dam thing off, so when it came to 'show-time', the first thirty minutes of the film were of his car seat and a lot of muttered swear words.

CHAPTER FOURTEEN

The field we had been allocated this year wasn't particularly ideal, punctuated with molehills and with only a small flat area to camp on. We were going to have to situate ourselves to the right of a fairly large slope, that ran down towards us and along the hedgerows that bordered the field, but they say beggars can't be choosers. So with our eye firmly on the weather we proceeded to set up camp, placing all the tents in a row along the line of the hedgerow.

Within our group of helpers, Akela had managed to commandeer a couple of members of the British Army. Dan Bailey as already mentioned and a chap called Alistair Irwin who held the rank of God or something.

Akela was chuffed that she had managed to convince these high-ranking officials to attend our little camp and was looking forward to the input they would no doubt have to offer. Something she wasn't aware of was that when you become an officer in the armed forces you never have to do anything for yourself again in your life. No more shoe polishing, no more cooking, no more arse wiping, no more nothing!!!. Some other poor sod spends his or her entire life doing it for you.

Using a bit of common sense wasn't particularly high on the agenda either. We had already witnessed this fact from Dan and his camcorder. But these men were obviously very intelligent people and in times of war, in which I thank God I have never been involved, the likes of these men would lead millions of soldiers into battle and hopefully magnificent victory. That is, provided they didn't have to think or actually do anything for themselves.

Akela had done well for helpers this year, probably remembering the year before when through working commitments all but Robert, Akela and myself had returned home after the Bank Holiday Monday. Not really a problem until you need to 'strike camp' on the Thursday. With this memory in mind and with typical 'Akela' overkill, she had nearly managed to volunteer more helpers than cub scouts.
Too many cooks, and not enough Indians, or something like that were causing a few problems. Thankfully, Robert had managed to delegate the duties of the camp to the slightly more experienced members. This left Dan and Alistair to break themselves in gently by allowing each of them to erect their own tent.

From Mafeking to Molehills

Tents that we had once again gratefully borrowed from Chafyn Grove.

"Those are exactly the same tents as they use in the army," said Robert as he peered over his shoulder to check on Dan and Alistair

"This camping lark should be a piece of cake for them," I said in reassurance.

"If they can't manage to put up a couple of tents, then who can?" I quipped as we pulled and tugged at yet another heavy canvas as it flapped and billowed in the westerly breeze that sometimes brought bad weather at this time of year.

The task of erecting the tents took the best part of the afternoon and by the time the boys had explored the surrounding areas and collected enough wood to start a fire, it was very nearly time to cook the evening meal.

It was at this point that we became aware that things weren't going too smoothly at the army end of our little camp. An awful lot of head scratching and finger pointing had been going on and very little else.

"Leave 'me to it," chuckled Robert, as it became more and more evident that the British Army was struggling a little with the fundamentals.

"It's getting a bit late," said Cathy realising we still had loads to do.

The Reluctant Cub Scout

"I think we ought to investigate and see what the problem is," suggested Trevor who, as always, was ready to tackle anything.

Everything that stood in front of us re-affirmed my suspicions about the structure of the armed forces. Although the likes of Montgomery and Churchill had got the praise, if it were not for the poor guys at the front end we would all be 'sprecken sie deutch' by now.

Much to their embarrassment and very much to our disbelief and amusement the two tents were standing; but only just.

"Bit of a problem with the poles," blurted Dan wanting to be the first with the excuses.

"You want to have a word with your supply chappy," moaned Alistair as he turned a little red more from frustration than embarrassment. "They've given us the wrong sized poles."

"Yes, can you believe it? I've had to spend hours adjusting the length of mine, it's bloody crazy," whined Dan as he pointed to his tent with the poles balanced precariously on a small pile of old bricks.

"Damn ridiculous if you ask me," Alistair blustered as he brushed away the dirt from his hands and placed the shovel against the poles that had been neatly planted a foot or so into the ground with little black piles of soil neatly patted around the base.

From Mafeking to Molehills

Robert stood looking from tent to tent for a while, chewing the bottom of his lip as he struggled for the right words to diplomatically express to this very bright pair that they ought to have talked to each other. Unable to bring himself to embarrass them in front of relative strangers, and realising that we were going to have a long camp; Robert just shrugged his shoulders and walked off. Cathy, Trevor and myself were a little concerned that the tents wouldn't survive the night but were assured by Robert that as soon as Dan and Alistair left camp to get the newspapers in the morning we would swap the poles over and erect their tents properly.

Our work continued as we set out the kitchen areas. Reluctantly the fire pits were dug a little closer than ideal to the tents but as we were restricted to the flat area of the field, they were going to have to do. For safety reasons several buckets of water were pulled conveniently from an old cattle trough that was lying unused and neglected half way up the slope of the field. These 'fire' buckets were placed next to each tent with the strict instructions to the boys not to touch or drink this water, as it was only to be used in an emergency. To be honest I think most of the cubs used them as pee buckets during the night because regardless of how many times they got knocked over in the malaise of camp there was always something in them. I suppose in the event of a fire anything would do.

Bob Harvey was a good friend of Akela and Robert. Along with his wife, Missy and their two young children, they had kindly given up a few precious days of their holiday to assist us at the start of cub camp. Bob began to express his concern about the vulnerability of the tents in the event of rain and suggested that we should dig V trenches in front of the tents to divert any rainwater that would inevitably run down the slope of the hill towards us. Within minutes and as if to prove Bob's theory right, it immediately started to pour with rain. Most of the cubs had either forgotten what it was like or had never camped in rain because nearly all of them were thinking it was great fun and were jumping about excitedly within their tents. They were splashing their feet about in the puddles that were quickly forming under the loose ground sheets that weren't adequate for the sort of downpour you can get in May.

The previous weeks had seen fine sunny weather firming up the ground nicely. This however only compounded the problem. The rainwater, which was now falling in stair rods, bounced off the hardened soil and flowed in muddy torrents down the slope towards us. Unchecked and unheeded it proceeded through the camp, completely swamping everything in its path including the tents before spewing through the hedgerow and into the neighbouring field.

The shower lasted for no more than a few minutes but by then the damage had been done. Nearly all the boys' sleeping bags that had been neatly placed on the ground sheets in their tents were now soaking wet along with rest of their possessions. Bob Harvey and a handful of others quickly started to dig the trenches that would, in the event of another storm, offer some sort of protection to the now sodden tents. And whilst this was being done Akela and I collected all the soggy sleeping bags and belongings and placed them in the minibuses, switched on the engines, revved them up and turned the heating systems on to full, blasting hot air into the buses. Within an hour everything was bone dry and beautifully warm, ready for use again. This ingenious lifesaving method of drying clothes has now been used on more than one occasion.

Thankfully the weather changed for the better, and the camp was blessed with sunshine for the rest of the week. So much so that I managed to go down with heat stroke on the

The Reluctant Cub Scout

Tuesday, after standing for a couple of hours in the midday sun without a hat on, patiently waiting for the boys to return from their search for clues during a treasure hunt. 'Mad dogs and Englishmen' and all that. But after a few hours with my feet in a bowl of icy water and a lot of T.L.C. from Akela, I was feeling better by the time supper was ready.

To make the best use of the limited space that we had, the eating areas were placed, on Robert's instructions I might add, slightly up the slope of the hill, a little away from the smoking fires and kitchens.

Ground sheets were arranged so that the six boys in each group along with a couple of the adults whose job it was to generally supervise and mark the points, could sit around these 'tables' and enjoy the welcome meal prepared and presented by the cubs themselves.

On this occasion Robert and myself were to eat together. Unusual in as much as Akela would normally separate the more experienced helpers and pair them up with an 'adult guest', for want of a better expression. As I had already survived a couple of cub camps, I was now becoming a fully fledged camper.

From Mafeking to Molehills

The supper for that evening was to be Spaghetti Bolognese. Not only mine but also Robert's favourite meal of cub camp. Fairly easy to cook and generally edible regardless of what the cubs had done to it.

In an effort to gain as many points as possible (a particularly difficult task when Robert or myself were marking), the group of cubs entertaining us for supper that evening had placed at the 'table' (this being a ground sheet laid on the floor) a couple of those awful chairs that had caused Mike Harrison so much grief and embarrassment a few years earlier. One at the head, facing up the hill and, luckily for me, one to the side.

Now, maybe I am being a little unkind, but with my devious ex-schoolboy mind and having witnessed what these little angels were capable of, something tells me that the events that happened next were too wonderful to have been an accident. And if, in fact, it hadn't been planned, it jolly well should have been. For whoever was responsible, and I'm still not sure who that was, I say a big thank you. I don't think I have seen anything quite so funny and have on many occasions, whilst attending a school function, which can at times be a little boring, managed to entertain and amuse new parents with the re-telling of the story of

The Reluctant Cub Scout

'Robert and The Spaghetti'. Even if it is only to show that there can be a funny side to Mr Cunliffe, the Headmaster.

In an effort to allow the cubs a little independence and to give them the feeling that they had prepared and cooked the meal unaided, most of the adults, after checking everything was under as much control as possible would gather in or around Akela's tent. This happened to be the only tent large enough to accommodate all the adults, and whilst we waited to be invited to join the boys for supper, would partake of a little refreshment. Normally this would consist of a couple of very large glasses of wine poured from a box that was always kept handy, but out of sight of the children.

After a lot of checking, correcting, and then more checking from our six, Robert and I were invited by a grinning cub who had amusingly slung a tea towel over his arm, waiter style, to join them for dinner. Robert at the head, of course, and once again thankfully, me to the side.

Serving food at camp, it must be said is never very easy, and is normally completed only after a lot of suggestions from either the 'Sixer' who was the boy in charge or sometimes, with the inevitable point deductions and moans from the boys, from the supervising adult.

The guest or guests would be served first. Then generally everyone else in some sort of pecking order. This quite often resulted in some poor little scrap looking woefully at an empty plate whilst the others gingerly balanced overflowing piles of spaghetti on their laps as they sat cross legged on the floor. After some juggling and redistribution of food, we would all bow our heads for Grace. Sometimes the right words in the wrong order but more often than not the wrong words in the wrong order, resulting in fits of suppressed giggles from the younger ones. However, provided it was near enough and not too blasphemous, they were allowed to start eating.

Robert, who likes his food, and ever eager to start after the fussing about, had after pulling rank on the redistribution of the food placed his plate which was now brimming with spaghetti and succulent meat covered in rivers of delicious tomato sauce, squarely on his lap. This was the only sensible way to eat when balanced on those ridiculous camping chairs. He lent back only just ever so slightly to allow the first tasty mouthful to slide blissfully down his throat. Now with the slope of the hill and the fact that he had his hands full, Robert could do nothing but stare straight ahead rigid in disbelief as he started to topple backwards on the chair. He landed it must be said, very gracefully, still in the seated position but firmly on his back. Followed a fraction of a second later by his somersaulting plate amazingly still full of spaghetti. Which landed by chance a few seconds later upside down, full in his face.......... Silence!

Never in all my years have I seen such self-control. Not from Robert, who was at this point drowning and gagging in spaghetti, but from the cubs who for fear of losing points or worse, had all bowed their heads and were staring at the ground in a monumental effort not to laugh. They continued to pretend that they hadn't noticed anything whilst slowly filling up with laughter, all bursting at the seams and making grunting and snorting noises in a desperate effort to control themselves. Well as you can imagine it was all too much for me and as I exploded with laughter the whole place just went up as if waiting for a signal. With the entire camp laughing hysterically, and all of the adults collapsing about in tears, it was without doubt one of the funniest sights I'd ever seen. Poor Robert who tried vainly to salvage some of his pride along with the rest of his dinner was staggering about with his head covered with long bits of spaghetti that dangled from his hair, like some cheap wig. Priceless !. If only Dan Bailey had had his camera rolling.

CHAPTER FIFTEEN

After the normal morning inspection and flag break, Akela had scheduled a walk around part of the estate. The idea was to let the cubs familiarise themselves with the surrounding area and interesting landmarks that existed here, so that these various points of reference could be used in the treasure hunt game that was to be played later that week.

With cubs of varying sizes and ages it was suggested that Akela should take the older boys who could walk slightly faster, along the longer route, by the old boathouse and approach some caves that were hidden in the woods from the north. Cathy and myself would walk the younger lads along the slightly easier path that passed by the folly.

It was suggested that all should take their torches to inspect the caves and we were all to meet at the entrance of the cave that was situated about half a mile from the campsite, a few hundred meters into the woods just south of the lake.

The boys had all been told to be careful when entering this part of the woods and to watch were they were going. This was because the area that housed the caves was continuously damp and slippery from a natural spring that ran under the estate, coming to the surface as it trickled down through the woods that sloped gently towards the lake. And not because of the cub eating bears that supposedly lived in the caves, according to 10th Camberley legend, made up by the older boys.

The light hearted banter about previous visits didn't help much either and Cathy and I innocently managed to stimulate their already active imaginations to bursting point as we enjoyed the early morning walk across the meadows.

 We ambled slowly towards the caves and looked forward to the day ahead as we crossed the carpeted fields of grass that lay patterned with the pastel shades of wild flowers. Each petal brightly punctuated by the diamond sparkle of the dew that seemed reluctant to evaporate under the warm attention of the ever welcome sun.

If the truth be known the caves were fairly disappointing, not very deep, a little smelly and full of discarded rubbish, but like most things in life the anticipation was normally better than the real thing. By the time we had arrived at the edge of the woods via the south and negotiated the wire fence that was protecting the area surrounding the caves, obviously to keep the bears in someone suggested, the younger boys' minds were beginning to run riot.

"Are you sure there are bears in the woods Mr Laidlaw?" asked Toby, who was a small skinny lad that had been holding my hand for part of the walk.

"Almost certainly" I replied with a wry smile.

"How big are they Mr Laidlaw?" he questioned as he looked up with large brown eyes that were opened just slightly wider than his mouth.

"Very big," I quietly whispered as if divulging a secret that no one else should hear.

"Bigger than Baloo?" he said, with reference to Kipling's bear in the story of the jungle book, and incidentally the name given to Akela's assistant.

"Probably the same size," I said beginning to regret that I started the whole conversation in the first place.

"Don't worry," I joked in an attempt to back out of this cul-de-sac "they're all probably out to lunch, and anyway, they'd eat me first. There's a lot more meat on my bones".

"Yes you're probably right" he reassured himself "but they might just use me as a tooth pick".

From Mafeking to Molehills

Akela and the older lads had hurried along the path of the boathouse, around the north side of the wood and had arrived at the caves several minutes before we had even reached the edge of the woods. They had already explored the caves and the carvings inside and got bored. A little disappointed, the older cubs, ever up to mischief, decided it would be fun to lay in wait and surprise the younger cubs as they entered the dark and dingy caves.

Great fun until you remember that Jonnie Boy here had spent the entire walk nonchalantly winding the poor little sods up, and had inadvertently added to the older boys' joke. Oblivious to the scheme the older boys had devised to brighten things up a little, and thinking it a tad strange that we hadn't seen them yet, we edged slowly towards the caves.

I told the youngsters to turn on their torches ready for when we entered the caves. Then thinking that perhaps Akela had managed to get herself lost or distracted I was unable to hold these eager youngsters back any longer, and allowed the smaller ones of our very excited group to enter the caves first.

Gingerly they stooped towards the opening, peering blindly into the endless dark, blinking as they tried to adjust their eyes to the gloom that lay ahead. Inch by inch they edged each other forward, ever closer, ever bolder. Ever braver these young explorers grew as they slowly entered the mouth. Step by step, they allowed the dark to envelop them; deeper and deeper they slowly entered the belly of the cave. "Roooaarr" came the blood curdling growls from the older boys who sprang from the darkest corners of the caves. Fingers shaped like claws that seem magnified by the shadows of the torchlight as they pounced on the horrified little scraps that had by now all turned in unison and stampeded back towards the mouth of the cave.

Pandemonium followed as they momentarily wedged themselves in the tiny entrance. Panic etched on their angelic little faces with the thoughts of what lay behind them. Screaming in sheer Terror, unable to move. They wriggled and jostled for what seemed like their lifetime in a desperate bid to free themselves from the clutches of the murderous cave. Finally bursting out into the relative safety of daylight and the woods beyond. Not once daring to stop or look back for fear of being eaten alive.

It would have been very funny if it hadn't scared the life out of most of them. I felt incredibly wicked about the smaller ones who had managed to wet themselves with fear and I spent the rest of the camp guilt ridden about my part in it all. Making daft comments about things living in caves whilst camping with eight year olds, was a little irresponsible to say the least. After a bit of mopping up we headed back across the meadows and followed the older boys who had run on ahead. Congratulating themselves on a successful mission and I would have to intervene before a scuffle broke out whenever they stopped to take the mickey out of some of the younger ones, still a little tearful from their scare.

Thankfully it was quickly forgotten by most of them and it still brings a guilty smile to my face every now and then. Needless to say the little ones gave the caves a very wide birth throughout the duration of the camp.

Bob Harvey in our absence and for the want of something better to do, had devised a game of 'camp golf'. Not as you would imagine the swinging of a golf club with a limp wrist, but the spacing out around the field of the small individual ground sheets normally used for sleeping on. The players throw a dinner plate 'Frisbee style' down the 'course' towards the 'greens', counting how many times it takes them before they hit the ground sheet. As in real golf the lowest score wins.

The Reluctant Cub Scout

The potential for fun was enormous, so much so that Akela decided to wait for the parents who were invited to 'visit' us on the Bank Holiday Monday, and hold a 'proper tournament' in the afternoon just after lunch.

The course was laid out in the adjacent field that was much lower than the campsite. The flag sticks were made from bamboo poles with large numbers crayoned untidily on bits of paper torn from an exercise book.

Willing parents who had arrived in droves and were still a little surprised to find that their precious son and heirs hadn't died from malnutrition or malaria, were now all happily herded into a group with an assortment of children. They were then divided into teams, given score cards, reminded that golf was a game played by gentlemen of honour and therefore no cheating was allowed and were led off to play the 'Tisbury Open' for 'big money prizes'..

From a grandstand view offered by the campsite, the spectacle of two dozen 'flying saucers' hovering around the countryside of Wiltshire, was enough to make anyone believe in crop circles. There were adults and children running around ducking and diving in an effort to miss any incoming discs that were flying menacingly towards them. Cries of 'FORE' resounded in the air as one bounced off the head of an unsuspecting parent before landing neatly onto the 'green'. Followed by the enormous whoops of joy at the scoring of yet another 'hole in one'

Robert, who had up until now been an amused spectator, became increasingly concerned for the safety of the children, and rightly so. He had realised the full potential and dangers of the wayward flying saucers, which by now were being hurled willy-nilly by almost every child in camp. He called a halt to the 'fun' and whistled everyone in for tea.

As we climbed the hill in a bubbling group of happy campers, all the children were jumping up like yapping spaniels demanding the results from Bob Harvey. He was trying to drag out the results as long as possible to give him time to reach the relative safety of the top of the hill before declaring the 'Tisbury Open' a draw. He burst out with laughter as he was bundled to the floor by the cheated boys before promising under a whole scrum of cubs that a rematch would be played as soon as Akela allowed.

We had learnt from many years of camping of the great advantage of having a younger adult along to help. They would not only save us older ones from back ache, but allowed us to leave the camp on certain occasions on prearranged trips in the safe and certain knowledge that the camp, although empty, was in capable hands. Generally they would be volunteered to dig pits, heave wood around and do all the jobs the more experienced helpers tried to avoid while they were out enjoying themselves. All this would be done under the guise of character building.

It was on one such occasion that we left Robin Greenwood. He was the teenage son of one of the teachers from school who had been sent along by his mother to help with the camp. Apparently Robin was attempting to join the R.A.F but for some reason was having trouble getting in, and it was felt that this experience could only help.

We set off on one of the various trips Akela had arranged, leaving Robin with instructions as to where to dig the latrine pit. We left in the comfort of knowing that from what we had already seen of Robin, the job would be well done. So it was with a little surprise that upon our return there was no sign of Robin. Just an enormous pile of rubble where the latrine pit was supposed to be.

From Mafeking to Molehills

We unloaded the cubs who then scattered into the woods like escaping convicts with the instructions to gather wood for their fires. Robert, Bob and myself wandered over to see if we could throw some light on where Robin might be hiding, obviously skiving off somewhere like most teenagers do when unsupervised.

As we approached we could hear faint grunting noises coming from the far side of the mound of earth that was seemingly getting bigger by the minute. We climbed to the top of the mound and peered open-mouthed into what was quite easily the largest and deepest hole I have ever seen dug by a single human being. It was at least ten feet deep and at the bottom was Robin, shirtless, covered in sweat heaving an enormous rock over his head onto the pile of earth that was now resembling a Welsh slag heap.

"I think you can stop now," explained Robert who was staggered at the sheer enormity and effort the lad had put into the task.

"That'll be deep enough," choked Robert. "Stop and have a rest."

"I think Akela has some drinks ready," Bob said as we turned towards the supply tent where Akela was waving a glass of something.

"Christ, did you see the size of that hole?" smiled Robert. "Bloody amazing!"

The Reluctant Cub Scout

"How far do you think he would have got?" I said, not quite believing that anybody could do that much work in such a short time.

"God knows. Probably Australia if we hadn't come back when we did," laughed Bob.

"He would have hit water first," joked Robert, always the teacher, and waited for a smiling Robin to catch us up.

"Come on let's get a drink," said Robert.
"I think I need one. I'm exhausted just thinking about it," I said.

CHAPTER SIXTEEN

The road to hell is paved with good intentions, or so I'm told. So it was with these apparently good intentions that Sam Collington volunteered to help us at cub camp one year.

Sam was a fireman who worked hard for the London Fire Brigade at Heathrow airport. Very impressive, as I imagine you don't get a much bigger fire than a jumbo jet laden with fuel. Not that Sam had actually put out a real aeroplane fire in his ten years of service. That said there is something comforting about having a fireman around when you are playing with fire in a field at a cub camp.

Now I have nothing but respect for all the services, firemen included but I wonder if you've ever noticed that when you dress somebody in a uniform, they get a little bossy and if that certain person isn't very tall, something even stranger happens.

Most people will tell you that they have experienced some hostility or aggression from a vertically challenged person. A friend of mine, who was tall to say the least, had experienced this reaction so many times that he had actually given this condition a name, calling it 'Short Man Syndrome'. Well, unfortunately,

The Reluctant Cub Scout

Sam our friendly Fireman was suffering from 'SMS.'

He was a nice enough chap but would carry a certain air about him. The strong and silent type. Believing in his own publicity. Regardless of what you did, he could have done it far better. He had to prove himself at every opportunity to anyone an inch or so taller than him, as if tall people really cared. We all have our crosses to bear but it seems that the small person's cross is larger and heavier and much more of a burden than anybody else's. We have all met the type at some point. Harmless enough but very, very, boring.

It probably didn't help that he fancied one of the mothers, who was a very tall, slim brunette, and if the truth be known, he probably only stuck up his hand and volunteered for cub camp to impress her son and therefore her.

Robert and Akela had spent many years ironing out the creases that come along with camping. A schedule and timetable would be drawn up and adhered to as closely as possible. Regrettably, somewhere along the way, somebody had forgotten to explain this to Sam.

From Mafeking to Molehills

God knows what he thought we did at camp. He probably carried the same misconception that most people have, and assumed that we sat round camp fires, singing 'Ging gang gooley'.

To his credit, Sam had spent the entire fortnight prior to cub camp planning and organising activities. Competitions that would not only last the full duration of camp, but were mind bending enough to confuse not only Robert and the rest of the adults, but our little eight year olds as well.

It was explained to Sam as gently as possible that the week would be based on our normal schedule of camping with the priorities of eating and sleeping paramount. However, if and when a 'window of opportunity' became available, he could take the boys off to compete in one of his planned activities.

Within his profession, Sam had obviously had an awful lot of training, with the emphasis on team building and trust. Most of the challenges and games revolved around these two fundamental points. The cubs seemed to enjoy most of the tasks that had, by now been spread all over the campsite. All but a few of the boys would eagerly take part. Although, it must be said, one of the activities went over the younger ones' heads, quite literally.

The Reluctant Cub Scout

As mentioned before, Ashley wood Farm is a working farm depending mainly on sheep for its income. This was quite handy for us, as the grass at the site was always kept short from the constant grazing.

Prior to our arrival we had been informed by the estate's office, who were ever grateful of any extra income, that a film was being made on one of the adjacent fields along by the lake. All very exciting for Akela as rumour had it that Johnny Depp was wandering around the town somewhere. The consequence of this was that grazing fields were at a premium and some of the sheep would have to stay with us!

The campsite itself was large enough to accommodate our woolly friends. So the farmer designated an area at the bottom of the field and this was neatly sectioned off with low voltage electric wire. The only downside to this was that it was very close to the only area suitable for one of Sam's games.

One of the challenges was for a team of six cubs whilst using two bits of string, and a set of numbers, along with an awful lot of luck to find some treasure that had previously been hidden within a large ten meter clock face drawn on the ground.

From Mafeking to Molehills

A boy would each hold an end of the string, stand around the edge of the clock face and move around the numbers as instructions were called out by the fifth member. The idea was, wherever the string crossed, the treasure would be found.

Now came the clever bit. In an effort to enhance trust and build character, Joe the sixth member of the team, who had until now, been paying very little attention, suddenly found himself with a London Fire Brigade smoke hood unceremoniously plopped over his head. Apparently these things were used in training to simulate the effects of a smoked filled room with total blackout.

The idea was for our little hooded wonder to follow the said pieces of string to where they intersected and start digging for the reward. So the little lad wandered around in total darkness, confused and bewildered not to mention petrified, whilst having his character built by being yelled at by every member of his team. It seemed to all those who were watching with mild amusement, a recipe for disaster.

Sure enough it wasn't long before confusion reigned with the members of the team getting bored, whilst some technical hitch was being sorted out. They had completely forgotten our little zombie with hands outstretched. Joe having been given no instruction for ages was now staggering aimlessly down the gentle slope towards the grazing sheep, and only coming to a halt when he stumbled blindly into the electrified fence.

Most of us have felt the jolt from this efficient farmers' fence. We have all been tricked by a sibling or goaded by a friend into touching the buzzing wire with a wet piece of grass or damp finger. Although painful enough, the voltage isn't that dangerous, but can you imagine the horror within this little lad's mind. Blindfolded against his will, screamed at by his mates, abandoned and now electrocuted. All for the sake of his character.

There was more fun to follow as his giggling team mates rushed to his aid only to jump backwards yelping in horror every time they touched the now "live" and electric Joe. Action needed to be taken. So with the help of a fairly large branch that had fallen during the night, and had somehow miraculously escaped the scavenging eyes of the cubs during that day's wood collection. I ran down the slope and started to prod poor Joseph's midriff with the end of the branch.

From Mafeking to Molehills

"Get off me" Joe squealed as I pushed and poke him in an effort to get him off the live wire and to relative safety.

"I don't want to play this game anymore, you're all mad" he screamed

Finally, after a few squeals and even louder screams as another jolt of electricity shot through his little arching body, Joe managed to roll over and over and off the now flattened fence. In an attempt to escape his torturers he blindly manoeuvred himself onto all fours and scampered off in the rough direction of the lake. On the way he managed to crawl headlong into a pile of sheep's muck that had no doubt been left there as some means of defence by one of the startled occupants of the adjacent field.

Not very impressed, Joe struggled to his feet whilst madly tugging to remove the smoke hood from his head. Tossing it to the ground he stormed off towards the relative security of his tent. Madly waving his arms in the air in disgust at the muck that had managed to attach itself not only to his hands and knees but also his very best tee shirt. Groaning as he attempted to wipe the offending stuff from his fingers. To add insult to injury, copious amounts of laughter from his so-called team mates accompanied him as he stomped up the hill.

The Reluctant Cub Scout

When Sam and I finally caught up with him he was muttering things about telephoning "Child Line" and reporting anybody and everybody to the authorities. With tears rolling down his cheeks from the injustice of it all, he had managed to convince himself that he would probably, or would almost definitely die from some mad sheep's disease or at the very least, smell for the entire duration of cub camp.

He was even more indignant at the fact that we couldn't stop smiling at him as he marched towards the campsite mumbling to himself about 'stupid silly games' and 'you wait until my parents find out'.

A little concerned I spent a full ten minutes assuring him that provided he washed his hands thoroughly, using lots of soapy water, (another injustice he would have to endure because his character apparently needed building); he was unlikely to catch anything too serious. This along with the advise not to bite his fingernails for a while and he would probably survive the rest of the camp with any luck. Another five minutes and I had convinced him to look at the funny side of things and had even managed to coax a smile from his tear stained face. This, along with a two-pound bribe to be spent in the tuck shop later that day, seemed to appease our little wounded soldier.

Thankfully nothing more was said and assuming that Joe did tell his parents they probably saw the funny side as much as we did.

CHAPTER SEVENTEEN

Lots of people have blind spots and I for one am no exception. Regardless of how many times you try to input the information, sometimes things just won't go in. With me it's spelling, no matter how hard I try I just can't fathom out whether it's 'passed' or 'past', 'there' or 'their', 'to' or 'too'. With Akela it was knowing her left from her right.

It would have been handy if I had discovered this at the beginning of my cub career. My sense of direction was such, that even when I was given the correct instructions I could stagger around the countryside for hours before I was lucky enough to bump into another 'six' a little less lost than I was. I would then tag onto them and follow just a few paces behind in the belief that they might know where they were going or, at the very least might lead me to wherever the rendezvous was supposed to be. For effect I would pretend to read the map and check the instructions before chasing after them as they sped off in an effort to lose me. Alternatively, they would deliberately spend ages leading me through narrow paths that ran between the thickets and brambles that grabbed at my legs and tore the skin from my arms as I tried to untangle the branches that clung to my clothes for all they were worth. I would shout at the boys to slow down before stumbling obliviously into icy cold streams or boggy marshland until I was waist deep in smelly water.

Akela would audibly tut when she saw me returning once again, from completely the wrong direction. In disbelief she would shake her head and ask why I had ignored her instructions which were quite clear and easy to follow and what was the point of her spending hours preparing these trails if I just went off and "Did my own thing, in my own little world.....blah, blah, blah".

Following Akela's instructions to anywhere was nigh on impossible. I was always too confused and just a little self-conscious to ever question her ability when the instructions given made absolutely no sense at all. After years of getting lost I began to wonder if it was all down to me. I carried the weight of embarrassment at always losing myself along with the cubs nearly every time we went out.

It always looked so good on paper.
'Follow the path for 500 paces then turn left up the track leading right to the horse jumps, then take the right fork towards the 'Wish Stream'. Turn right, walk for 300 paces then left at the cross roads at the next junction turn left ....

The Reluctant Cub Scout

On one occasion, always assuming that it would all become clear along the way, I, along with a handful of cubs, blindly set off only to scratch our heads at the very first junction. We stared for ages at the instructions looking for a left hand path that didn't exist. Just the opposite. Within a few hundred yards of setting off we were lost. Stumped at the very first intersection and from there on in, everything turned to worms as normal!

Thankfully Akela was sussed out. Prior to one of the cub camps she had sent the itinerary for the week, along with explicit instructions on how to get to the campsite, to the regional Scout Headquarters. We were quite often visited by the local scout commander or inspector during camp week and the directions were sent to help them find us parked in a field somewhere, miles from habitation.

Obviously a dedicated man, and not to be put off lightly, the inspector followed Akela's instructions meticulously, only to find himself retracing his steps when completely lost. Time after time he set off assuming incorrectly that for some reason he was getting it wrong and returned to his starting point. Having spent all day Saturday and most of Sunday wandering around Tisbury, he had made this inspection a personal quest. He only faltered when he passed the 'Beckford Arms' for the third time and finally succumbed to the thought of a nice cool beer.

Fortunately for him, his idle chatter with the publican led to the discovery that there was in fact a group of cubs camping in a field at the bottom of the lane, just visible from the car park. If he waited long enough, the landlord informed him, he was sure to spot a couple of the cubs aimlessly wandering around on some treasure hunt or something with pieces of paper in their hands, scratching their heads as they read the instructions.

"I know how they feel," remarked the inspector.

"Just follow those two," said the publican as he pointed to a couple of cubs who had just appeared through a hole in the fence by the lane and were running down the track towards the campsite like a pair of frightened foxes running from the pack.

"It'll be like the blind leading the blind," one of the locals joked as the inspector hurried out of the bar in hot pursuit of the boys. Cursing wildly as he bumped his head with an audible crack on the frame of the tiny doorway as he left the pub.

"Told you," said the smug beer drinker as he went back to his pint and watched in mild amusement at the inspector as he trotted across the road dropping paperwork whilst dodging the traffic as he chased the boys who were disappearing down the lane.

"Would you care to explain this?" he asked in all his officialdom as he waved a tatty piece of tyre stained paper marked 'Directions' under Akela's nose. He milked the silence as Akela struggled in search of the words adequate to explain in simple terms what she meant...

"When one says left, one could possibly have meant right, and when one means right, right, one could have meant left;"

At last after all the years of cringing and having the embarrassment of having to explain to Akela that I'd got lost again, it was suddenly all becoming clear. Smiling, I watched as she dug herself in deeper and deeper.
"Go on," I goaded "explain that again to the nice inspector," remembering the years of self-doubt. "I don't think he's quite got it yet."

Akela slowly repeated her explanation.

"Right so when you say left it doesn't necessarily mean you mean left, does it, you could mean right, right?
"Right." She smiled her confirmation as if he had finally got it.

"And when you say right, right; you mean left, right."

"Sometimes."

"Right." He nodded already beaten and confused.

"Right, not so hard was it?" she sighed glad that all the confusion was nothing to do with her.

"Now we've cleared that up would you like a drink inspector?" she smiled giving him one of her 'silly little man' looks normally reserved for me.

"No thanks, I've got a cracking headache," he said wincing as he rubbed the lump on the top of his head.

"Don't suppose you've got an aspirin in the first aid box by any chance?"

"Of course we have," beamed Akela "it's in the supply tent. Just over there on the Righ-eft".

CHAPTER EIGHTEEN

Like most cub packs that made a visit to the south coast or more specifically to the area around Poole, an excursion to where it all began was very nearly compulsory.

Over the years 10th Camberley had made this pilgrimage many times. We would pass the queues of cars that sat patiently along the busy tree lined avenue, which was heavily scrawled with double yellow lines that twisted in unison as it suddenly led to the dead end that marked the terminus.

Their occupants were silently resigned to the inevitable delays of the bank holiday traffic. They all waited in turn, understanding the chaos caused by the small capacity of the little chain ferry that trundled endlessly across the waters to Studland in a relentless struggle to appease the hoards of day trippers.

The pay point was a small wooden kiosk brightly painted in the corporate colours of the small ferry firm that managed to scrape a living from necessity. Tickets were sold here not only to Studland but also for various trips around the bay, including our destination, Brownsea Island.

From Mafeking to Molehills

Robert and I offloaded Akela, Cathy and the boys at the small ticket office and drove the mile or so to find the nearest empty car park. We walked back past the individually designed houses that were set well back from the road behind fortress like walls, with their glazed green and blue roof tiles, that were fashionable in the twenties, but now looked oddly out of place. The gardens that surrounded these architectural masterpieces were as elegant as the structures themselves, with perfect lawns that ran parallel to the water's edge.

The shuttle service that ran across to the island was adjacent to the chain ferry and left at half hourly intervals. With the last one leaving Brownsea at four thirty in the afternoon, I often wondered what would happen to the stragglers who missed the last boat home. This scenario must have occurred on numerous occasions as the walk, which was the only way around the island for visitors, took forever.

Thankfully 10th Camberley never found themselves in the predicament of having to swim home. Apparently this was the only option left open to latecomers, according to the National Trust steward who greeted our little troop when we invaded his island.

The Reluctant Cub Scout

"Make sure you're back by four," he yelled as we marched off towards the park area that seemed to be home for most of the island's wildlife.

"Hey Morgan, there's your mother" shouted one of the boys as he pointed to a brightly coloured peacock strutting in full display.
"That's a male you idiot," advised Robert harshly.
"Sorry Morgan, apparently it's yer dad," he said ducking the retribution from Robert as he chased the bird away.

Akela was delighted to find so much free space in what was after all a designated picnic area and suggested we settle down on the exceptionally short grass and eat our lunch. Surprised but grateful for the lack of crowds, she rummaged through the cardboard boxes carried over by the older boys whilst Robert and myself fended off the unwanted attentions of a couple of nosy geese. Their sole purpose was to keep the grass short, Robert informed me and I was working out how to smuggle one home for the lawn when it crapped on my foot.

Spreading out the limited selection of goodies as best she could, Akela instructed the cubs to shuffle past, buffet style, whilst helping themselves to whatever they fancied. Starving as always, the boys jostled each other as they stuffed their sandwiches so full that they had little chance of eating them before the fillings plopped to the ground.

As the contents somersaulted ground-wards the audible groans from the boys were masked only by the squawking acceptance from most of the island's wildfowl to join them for lunch.

In an open invitation the ducks, geese and peacocks charged towards us as they stampeded out of the woods from every direction, pecking and prodding at anything that slightly resembled food.

It was carnage. There were birds flapping and flailing as the cubs jumped and screamed as their attackers madly pecked around their feet. Stumbling in panic, the boys charged through the melee of birds, hotly followed by Akela, Cathy, Robert and myself.

Desperately we scooped up as much as we could carry, abandoning most of our picnic to the scavenging flocks. By the time we caught up with the boys we were wading knee deep in bird life as the gaggle followed our every move.

To avoid fatalities on either side we started to throw what was left of our lunch over the heads of the marauding masses in the hope that the chasing pack would be diverted long enough for us to make our escape.

Inch by inch we edged our way across the grass, tiptoeing towards the crowds that had now gathered along the wooded fringe of the park to view the spectacle of 10th Camberley cub pack getting pecked to death.

Disappointed that we had no more to offer, the birds redirected their attentions towards another unsuspecting group. Some people who had settled down to enjoy a nice quiet picnic seemingly surprised to find lots of space in such a suitable area.........

Guilty for not warning them but grateful for the distraction, we grabbed the opportunity and hurried off across the park to continue the walk towards our goal.

From Mafeking to Molehills

'This stone
commemorates the
experimental camp of
20 boys held on this site
from 1st-9th August 1907 by
Robert Baden Powell
Later Lord Baden Powell
Of Gilwell
Founder of the scout
and guide movements'

Like most great journeys they started with one small step. I stood and wondered what the reaction would be today if someone had suggested taking twenty young men off to the country to camp. Thankfully Baden Powell had the courage and foresight to deal with whatever prejudice he faced, with millions of young people in hundreds of countries now benefiting from his ideals.

My personal belief is that the foundations laid for young people when attending cubs, brownies and subsequently scouts and guides, are carried with them throughout their lives. We ask them to make a promise, and ask them to do their best. We ask them to think of others before themselves possibly for the first time. As a group we ask them to work for each other rather than as individuals, surely not a bad thing in today's society.

Few remember their time spent scouting as a negative experience. Most learn a great deal not only about the practical side of life but also about themselves and I believe that very few have regrets. All except my daughter of course, who resigned from the brownies in protest at having her 'Care Bear' surgically opened up to remove the mechanical talking devise that was keeping the rest of the pack awake at brownie camp while she rolled around in her sleep.

We continued our stroll around the island and began to realise that having reached our objective there was very little else to keep us amused. We ambled down the tarmac paths towards nothing in particular. The highlight was trying to spot red squirrels that apparently lived on the island but had cunningly avoided revealing themselves to 10th Camberley.

The boys were getting bored and to be honest with you the adults weren't far behind. It was all just a little bit of an anticlimax and to cap it all, it had started to rain. Maybe it was a test or perhaps we had angered the god of camping or something. Here we were miles from anything that resembled shelter and we had managed to bump into a thunderstorm.

From Mafeking to Molehills

Reluctantly we huddled under one of the huge oak trees that lined the way. Not clever under the circumstances but having arrived in bright sunshine we weren't dressed to combat such a downpour. It was declared that we were more likely to catch our deaths than get struck by lightning so we sheltered as best we could under the dark canopy.

The more the rain fell the more porous our shelter became. The only really dry place was under the large trunk that bent slightly at an angle as it grew into branches. To no-one's surprise, Robert pulled rank, and managed to muscle his way under the dry trunk, before snuggling as close to the tree as was humanly possible. Avidly he defended his spot with his elbows as soon as anyone dared to venture too close. The rest of us were left to fend for ourselves and, unable to find another dry spot, stood motionless while the rain did its worst.

We were all wringing wet and slowly steaming, not only from the rain that was evaporating under the return of the sunshine but because Robert couldn't understand what all the moaning was about or why we were so fed up.

We set off drenched and uncomfortable as we sloshed down the waterlogged track that eventually led us back to the harbour. Robert meanwhile, completely dry, was enjoying the stroll and suggested that maybe we should have sheltered under the tree as he had.

To add insult to injury I started sneezing, probably from a cold that had been threatening for a couple of days but had now been unable to resist the timing. 'Just great,' I thought as we returned to the jetty and souvenir shop that was strategically placed in such a way that you had to walk past it to board the little bobbing boat.

"Would you like a memento of the visit?" Akela suggested as she strode over to the shop that was now crammed full of very damp cubs.

"Err no dank you, Akela I dink I'll forget diss one if you don't mind," I sniffed and went off to sulk in the boat.

CHAPTER NINETEEN

"It appears Wales is for sale" said Robert as we trundled past yet another empty pub flanked by rows of untidy houses with 'For Sale' boards that stood like flags with rigor mortis.

"Yes, it does seem a little quiet. Probably all off chasing sheep or something," I thought out loud as we pulled the Volvo into the car park of a hopeful looking pub called the 'Cock and Pullet'.

Robert had promised me a succulent lunch, provided we got the dry shelter tents up before one o'clock. We had been working like Trojans in an effort to beat the rain, rain that was compulsory in this part of the world or so I'm told. But after completing our task with expert ease the lunch bit was proving to be a little difficult to track down.

Apparently all the men in Wales were professional drinkers, second only to Welsh women. This was contrary to my beliefs but had been confirmed on many occasions by a close friend of mine who came from these parts.

Strange then that we found the 'Cock and Pullet' surprisingly empty.
"Maybe it'll get busier later on, they probably have different working hours to us," I said to

The Reluctant Cub Scout

Robert as he ordered a couple of pints and some 'Pub Grub' from a chalk board menu that was hanging by its corner from the yellowing ceiling. A menu I might add that had been slightly altered by the local wag and read 'Plough my Crotch' and 'Nipple Pie'. Very apt for the 'Cock and Pullet' I thought and probably the only entertainment the inhabitants ever got around here.

"Where will you be sitting my lovelies?" asked a well-rounded lass from the valley who managed to fill most of the area behind the bar. "Just so as I can find you, when I bring the food out, you know," she said smiling with bored politeness.

"Err, over there," replied Robert, slowly looking around the bar in an effort to find the crowds of people we had obviously missed when we came in.

After thoughtfully surveying the rows of unoccupied seats in the completely empty pub, Robert wandered slowly over towards the fire, that in a strange sense of irony was burning brightly from coal imported from Newcastle. Or so it said on the bag.

Still wondering whether we had missed something, we selected a table by the window and peered out though the grimy glass in the vain hope that we might spot someone or something as they passed by the window, if only to confirm that we weren't alone in Wales.

"Have you ever noticed that you have to pay to get into Wales, but they let you escape completely free of charge" mused Robert. "I wonder why."

The food was pleasantly tasty, bearing in mind it had been freshly cooked from a plastic bag taken from the freezer. I wondered what part of the microwave chips came into the description of 'Home Made Fare' as advertised on the wall outside. But it was served attentively by the landlady who tried unsuccessfully to keep herself busy whilst listening to our conversation.

Rain had started to fall again and as Robert and I had no particular desire to hurry back to school, we sat in the pub and slowly sipped our beer. Eventually, from the subtle hints coming from the bar area, it became obvious to us that the lunchtime session was over. Most of the lights in the pub were or had been turned out, probably in an effort to save money more than a signal for us to leave.

As we walked back to the car, I wondered how anybody ever made a living in Wales. We hadn't seen anybody else in the pub, and had probably doubled, if not trebled the entire turnover for the day. The bill itself including the beer came to a little over thirteen pounds. No wonder everybody in Wales wants to sell their place.

We crossed the Severn Bridge as we headed 'back to Blighty'. I scanned the distant horizon for a view of the huge concrete footings that were being erected for the new Severn Bridge. Or should it be the Eighth? How on earth do they get the concrete to set under water, in the middle of an estuary I thought, as we made our way along the rain soaked motorway, windscreen wipers slopping as they struggled to make an impression on what was now torrential rain.

Thankfully by the weekend the weather had improved and as Robert and I collected the minibuses early on Saturday morning from a local van hire company, the sun was actually shining. Probably trying to lull us into a false sense of security.

Collecting the minibuses was a job neither of us particularly looked forward to or enjoyed. The chap who ran the business was probably the most miserable human being I have ever come across.

From Mafeking to Molehills

In the ten years that we have been using the firm I have never seen him happy. Christ if he truly doesn't like his job that much, he should change it. Maybe he should become a traffic warden or a wheel clamper and then he could be a really professional miserable bastard.

But year after year Mr Grumpy is there. Grudgingly he slams the necessary paperwork down on the counter, as he asks me to sign here, here and here, without even looking at me. I scrawl nervously in what I hope is the correct place, not daring to ask him to repeat his instructions.

God knows what would happen if I had got it wrong and I shudder to think of the consequences if he had had to start the paperwork all over again. I always left the place feeling as if I had personally upset him in some way. Probably just by being there I suppose. Still the minibuses are reliable enough and that's what really matters.

After the normal Saturday commotion of loading the van and getting the cubs seated into the correct minibus, we set off west towards the motorway and Wales. Akela had long since made sure that any cub likely to misbehave was parked tightly into the bus that Robert would be driving.

The journey was a long one by our normal standards and we had pre-arranged a stop at the service station beside the Severn Bridge. This would give the boys an opportunity to stretch their legs and their minds as they surveyed the magazines on sale that were meant for the lorry drivers, before joining the longest queue in the world for hamburgers and chips.

Obviously everyone assumed that they weren't going to get fed until they returned to England. Maybe they just thought that the hamburgers in Wales were made from sheep droppings or something, because much to Robert's frustration we waited half an hour for the boys to be served. Then a further twenty minutes for them to be gathered from various parts of the service station before we could continue our journey towards Llanvair Discoed and our camp site.

The land we were to camp on was owned by Richard Micklethwaite. He was the uncle of a boy that Robert had taught many years before at Chafyn Grove. Sadly it seemed Richard had lost most of his money in the Lloyds insurance fiasco of the late eighty's (being one of the names), but was refusing to give it to them. Good for him, I say.

Like a lot of people under enormous strain, alcohol was very much a crutch for Richard, and with the uncanny timing that all drinkers seemed to have, he would trundle down to our camp site, beeping his horn to scatter the sheep, just as we opened the wine for supper.

Richard would explain with great glee that he had spent most of his entire life changing all the footpaths and rights of way that were on his land and clearly marked on all the maps, "Just to muck up all the ramblers," as he so nicely put it. Not to mention a completely bemused and helpless cub pack, but that's another story.

After gulping down several very large glasses of wine, followed by two or three tins of my own private supply of premium lager, Richard slurred a thank you towards us. Akela, not very discreetly and looking as suspicious as hell, then handed him a large bottle of Teachers wrapped in a brown paper bag. To an outsider the scene would have looked like some illegal payment or bribe, rather than a gift for the use of a field.

The Reluctant Cub Scout

Richard would then attempt to negotiate the field, sheep, tents, stream, hedges, woods and whatever else got in his path as he made his way up the valley towards his magnificent stately home. All this whilst accompanied by his trusty black Labrador who would sit, girlfriend like, in the front passenger seat of his ten year old land Rover.

The vehicle had the baldest tyres I have seen outside a racing circuit, and had probably never been close to a garage, (not even for fuel as apparently he ran it on farm diesel) let alone passed an M.O.T inspection. A little worrying really, but as Richard said "All perfectly bloody legal on my own land old chap, and anyway what ever wildlife I run over and kill, I eat."

"Really? Does that include cub scouts?" I enquired a little concerned.
"Almost definitely, but I'm not sure I could manage a whole one," he laughed.

CHAPTER TWENTY

The landscape that surrounds Llanvair Discoed is magnificent. The forests stretch in all directions bar the south from where the Severn estuary has managed to cut its muddy borders through the low flat countryside, bringing its cold murky water, deep and foreboding, inland as it churns towards the city of Bristol.

In hard contrast the deep green pines that were deliberately planted many years beforehand, stand to the north east and west of the campsite in neat and tidy columns. Chameleon in their behaviour, these fields of lumber were forever changing colour as the beams of light swept across the canopy in a kaleidoscope of yellows and greens. Rejoicing in the warmth each time the sun broke through the seemingly ever-present clouds. Clouds that were now starting to build menacingly from the west. These elegant forests stretched slowly at first along the gentle slopes that rolled along the edge of the valley, then rose steeply skywards, giving the landscape a sharp definition as the dark green tree line touched the horizon.

Armed with a map and compass, Akela had made the decision to walk the boys up through the forest in a rough north westerly direction. Not just an aimless amble as is our norm, but in search of a huge hydro electric dam that was shown on the map and that had now been clearly marked out with a large red circle from a biro.

"Now, provided we follow the footpaths that are clearly signed, we should have absolutely no trouble in finding our objective," stated Akela. She was flapping the map in the general direction of the trees and ignoring the groans from the cubs who had been promised an adventure, not a five mile hike.

"And," she went on, "provided we walk quickly it should only take us about an hour or so." No problem.

I think most people find map reading difficult. In principle, and even in theory, it should be easy, but it isn't. It also doesn't help if you leave without checking where you are, or more importantly, where you are starting off from before charging off in a flurry, full of excitement like a herd of running cub scouts. Pursued by a gaggle of wheezing adults, who in an attempt to catch them up find to their horror that the gently rolling hills of Wales aren't so gentle.

From Mafeking to Molehills

We continued to march confidently along the footpaths and into the cool atmosphere of the pines. We entered the edge of the forest and headed in a northerly direction up the hill towards a ridge that was approximately two miles from our campsite.

We took a rest and looked down onto our tented village that was nestling tidily within the lush green valley down below and could just make out Robert who was busying himself around the camp whilst taking full advantage of the solitude.

The walk had been compulsory and some of the really young ones were already starting to grumble. This was not surprising as the slope had now turned into a fully blown hill, steep enough to be shown on the map as lots of squiggly lines in circles, apparently called contours.

By this time Akela had become bored with having to read the map and promptly handed the map and compass to David Craig, who along with his wife Hilary, had accompanied us to this year's camp. It might have been prudent if someone had actually bothered to ask David if he could read a map.

The Reluctant Cub Scout

I was grateful that the task hadn't been given to me. I suppose Akela knew me all too well and had already decided that although always willing, my sense of direction and therefore my map reading skills were, to say the least, appalling and that David or in fact anybody, would do a better job than I would.

According to David, after a fleeting consultation with the map, and always assuming we had followed the correct footpaths that helpfully pointed the way, the dam should have been found just over the next ridge.

We stumbled hurriedly towards the top, expending more energy than was wise in an effort to be the first to spot the dam and win a 'A Big Money Prize' promised by Akela. The boys scurried up the slope in a race and stood facing away from us in the direction they had been running.

Spellbound no doubt by the majestic beauty of the deep blue waters being forcibly held back by the awesome structure carved from stark grey concrete... Wrong. Trees, lots and lots of trees.

Confused, the adults surrounded the map and looked, waiting for a now flustered David to say something. Silence, a few umm's and ahh's but other than that, nothing.

Now it's probably a little harsh to say that David had managed to get us lost. The fact that Akela had shoved the map at him before continuing to walk off at her unmatchable pace left David with little chance of getting his bearings. If the truth be known Akela was probably lost before she handed responsibility over to the poor unsuspecting helper. But lost we were.

"You can't just lose a dam," Hilary blurted in a tone that suggested that David had done it on purpose. "You wouldn't have thought so," I chipped in, trying to deflect David's growing embarrassment.

"I think it's a little farther on," he said. "Yes definitely," he confirmed with growing confidence.

Now call me mister sceptic, but having searched the horizon as far as the trees would allow and assuming that trees don't grow on water, where the hell could four hundred, million gallons of Welsh water be hiding? Because I'll be dammed if I could see it, if you'll excuse the pun.

The Reluctant Cub Scout

It was at this point that the rain started. Firstly as a light drizzle slowly searching all the exposed pieces of clothing for the chinks. It soon turned into torrents of water that forced its way down the back of our necks, only stopping at the underwear just long enough to make it one of the most uncomfortable feelings I have ever experienced.

We were lost, fed up and very wet. The younger ones were now close to tears with the older boys starting to misbehave. We had walked in excess of five miles uphill and still had no real idea of where we were or where the damned dam was.

We had set off just after lunch and although daylight wasn't a factor we had been gone for nearly three hours. Now, assuming we could find the right direction towards home this would presumably also take a few hours, and with this in mind we abandoned our search for 'The Lost Dam" and turned round and round and round.

Another hour passed as we followed the footpaths that would appear from nowhere and were certainly not shown on any map, but logic had it that if they were there, they must lead somewhere, so we followed them.

From Mafeking to Molehills

We took a path that entered a field guarded by a bullock that inquisitively ambled after us, sniffing the air as if lunch had arrived. Slowly he gained speed the faster we tried to walk away from him.

Furtively looking back we hurriedly started to cross the rain sodden field, finally breaking into a sprint that was only slightly faster than the now galloping beast.

Thankfully and to our good fortune we were able to find safety around an old rusty combine harvester that had either been dumped or had broken down many years beforehand.

Thirty-eight soaking wet bodies slowly edged around this monstrous machine in some lopsided rugby scrum whilst the snorting opposition, steaming from the rain, stared at his prey and stood his ground.

"What the hell do we do now?" I groaned, concluding that this was by far the best lost I had ever been.

"Shoo it away or something," demanded Akela as if the 'something' was so obvious that she was surprised we hadn't thought of it already.
"What do you suggest?" I asked, noting that the animal looked as pissed off as I was.

"I don't know; wave a red rag at it or something."

"I think we've already got its attention Akela, thank you very much," I mused trying desperately to remember if bullocks were meat eaters.

"Shoo, go away; go on, shoo, shoo!" Akela shouted plucking up enough courage to edge forward ever so slightly before scampering back around the derelict iron structure and into ankle deep water that was now accumulating under our squelching feet.

"I'm not sure it understands English, being Welsh and all." I said as I looked to the ground to avoid the beasts gaze as it dribbled mucus from its flaring nostrils.

It was at this point that I noticed Hilary's footwear, or lack of it. She was holding in her left hand a pair of fairly expensive white Gucci shoes now splattered in mud and in her right, a pair of diamond earrings or should I say one diamond earring.

Some people have no idea!

"I've lost my bloody earring" she whined, looking at the floor as she hopped from one foot to the other in the hope that she might find it. She stared hatefully at the dark gluey mud that was sucking at her feet only to see it seep through her toes like some grotesquely twisting worm whenever she placed her foot back on the ground.

"Jesus, David, get me out of here," she screamed.

"Oh, right then" he huffed. "Abra-bloody-cadabra," he shouted as he stormed off, resigned to the fact that according to his now dishevelled wife, Akela, myself and thirty four cub scouts it was definitely all his fault.

This was just the break we needed. Our ever attentive farm friend started to follow David, who by now couldn't have given a toss whether he was mauled to death or killed by nagging, and had walked off dejectedly towards the boundary of the field in a effort to escape his now hysterical wife.

Disappearing through a gate he suddenly screamed "dry land!" a little more enthusiastically than he would have wished.

"A road I mean. Civilisation. We're safe, saved, oh thank you, thank you, thank you," and started to danced a jig along the narrow but solid roadway.

Free from our captor, who had lost interest some time ago, we wearily trekked along the man made road until we found a sign pointing towards Llanvair Discoed, telling us that 'home' was only four miles and roughly one hour's walk away!

Fuelled by the thought of dry clothes, food and warm shelter we set off in the direction that the signpost had advised. Thankfully this one had not been moved by Richard Micklethwaite 'just to mess up the ramblers' and after an hour's hard slog we marched or should I say stumbled into camp. Five hours late. "Where on earth have you been?" quizzed Robert, a tad flustered.

"Err we got a little lost," replied Akela as she stared hawk eyed at the strange tubby man wandering around her campsite. He was writing notes on a clipboard as he suspiciously prodded and poked at the canvas before tugging at one of the ropes that was meant to be holding up a tent.

"Who's that?" she queried nodding towards the intruder, her protective instincts kicking in as her hackles rose.

"Scout Inspector for Camping and he wants to know why you've tried to drown the kids," joked Robert as he strode over to introduce Akela to Mr Bumble or whatever his name was from Divisional Head Quarters

From Mafeking to Molehills

"Nice to meet you," she lied as she wiped the residue from the handshake down the back of her skirt.

"I've been watching you for a couple of days," he said a little scarier than Akela was comfortable with and waited in silence as he checked the various notes entered on the clipboard. "I live up on the hill over there. You can just see my place if you look hard enough through those trees."

"I've been using my binoculars to check you lot out. Very good, very good indeed," he announced and placed his arm across Akela's shoulder as he shepherded her towards the supply tent.

"Is this where you keep the booze?" he enquired spying the bottle of whiskey that we normally gifted the farmer for the use of the land.

"Medicinal purposes only you understand," retorted Robert who by now had got the measure of our little Welsh inspector.

"Would you like some?"

We stood and chatted while the boys built their fires and I was thankful that the remnants of rain were moving quickly across the Severn towards the east into England. At least this allowed the cubs to prepare the dinner and show the nice Mr Inspector that we knew roughly what we were doing.

The Reluctant Cub Scout

All our Mr Bumble wanted to do was drink our Scotch. By the time dinner was served he was very nearly legless and was telling all who cared to listen as we ate that he was in the Welsh Cave & Mountain Rescue Service. The best part of the job is when they take parties of teenage girl's potholing.

Apparently before the girls are allowed to enter the caves the Welsh Cave & Mountain Rescue Service would insist on taking the girls' bras off. Whether they helped them with it or let the girls undress themselves was never really made clear but the story had certainly got Robert's attention, who was now all ears.
"What on earth would you do that for?" he asked
 "Well you see, it's all to do with the wire."
"What wire?"
"The wire in the bras," he smirked.
"We have to check them to make sure that there isn't any."
"Why?"
"Because they get stuck."
"Who do?"
"The girls do."
"How?"
"They snag."
"On what?"
"The rocks."

"How?"

"The bras."

It was like watching a tennis match.

"Why?"

"The wire under the bra."

"Oh."

"Yer, the larger they are the bigger the problem."

"Sure."

Forty, thirty...

This was still going on when I left to check the boys and wondered what the point was of sending these people to check up on us. It seemed from the conversation I had just heard that most of the checkers needed checking.

By the time nightfall arrived Robert had managed to pour Mr Bumble into the back of the Volvo and was heading out of the campsite to take him home.

I watched just mildly amused as the car suddenly screeched to a halt as Robert hopped out, trotted round to the rear passenger side opened the door and jumped backwards in an effort to avoid the remains of Mr Bumble's dinner. God! It had been a long day, and no, we never found the dam.

CHAPTER TWENTY ONE

One of the plus points about camping in Wales was that Akela had contacted a couple of local activity centres. This would be ideal for the boys to try something a little different from the usual camping excursions. Excitement mounted as the cubs learnt from Akela that pony trekking was to be on the agenda.

On the Sunday of camp, because the number of ponies was limited, we split ourselves up into two groups. One for the morning ride, and one for the afternoon session. We set off with the first group to the waves and cheers from the boys we had left behind and headed towards the riding centre that had foolishly accepted our booking.

I have never fully understood the attraction of horses and struggle to grasp why so many people seem to enjoy them so much. They have big teeth, large feet, huge arses, and they smell, and that's just the people that ride them. Neither was my favourite animal by any means and I told myself that in order to keep any credibility with the boys I would have to bullshit, or should I say horse shit, my way through the next couple of hours.

From Mafeking to Molehills

Trevor, who had once again volunteered for cub camp, was proudly explaining to anyone who would listen, which wasn't many, that he had a friend in America who was a real life sheriff. Not only that, but the belt, hat and boots he was wearing were all 'genuine' cowboy's gear and had been given to him by 'Billy the Kid' or someone.

What the hell that had to do with pony trekking in Wales was beyond me, but he must have felt that wearing these clothes and singing "Home on the range" would in some way confirm him as 'Roy Rogers' or somebody.

Anyway either the minibus was bugged or the people running the centre had got the measure of Trevor as soon as they set eyes on him. That, or there really is a God.

The truth was that Akela had once again managed to get her numbers wrong, failing to include some of the adults in her calculations when she'd returned the booking form.

"We seem to have a problem," explained one of the handlers to Robert, who by now was counting heads in an attempt to make things tally.

"We got sixteen ponies ready as you instructed sir, but you've got seventeen riders in the first group," he murmured, as he wiped the back of his neck with his hanky, mimicking deep thought.

"Couldn't you find something, just this once, just to help us out" pleaded Robert, who was very reluctant to upset anyone by telling them that they would have to miss the ride because his wife couldn't count.

"I'll see what I can do sir," smiled the helpful assistant who had probably set the whole thing up for the amusement of his staff in the first place.

As Robert and I stood as far away from the clopping hooves as possible, the cubs filed out, one by one in an orderly procession of horsemen, all neatly kitted out with smart riding helmets and beaming smiles of anticipation.

"Where's Roy Rogers then?" shouted one of the girls who was checking the saddles and girths around the boys' ponies.

"He'll be with you in a minute," giggled one of the stable lads who had just appeared from helping Trevor organise himself at the back of the main stables.

Imagine the scene. Here we have someone who is apparently just about to be shot out of a cannon, whilst balancing a helmet that is at least six times too small for him perched perilously on the top of his head. He sits astride an animal that could only be loosely described as a pony. Its back bent, its belly bulging, as the rider's feet drag along the ground, scraping the toes of his highly polished 'genuine cowboy boots'. Then basically you've got the picture. An absolute classic stitch up.

Robert managed to drop the camera because he was laughing so much and I would have joined in a little more heartily, if I hadn't been aware of having to return for my session later that day.

The pony Trevor was to ride, had until then, been happy to graze the lush green pastures of retirement. Dobbin as he was referred to, was pretty miffed at having had his lunch interrupted and regardless of what Trevor wanted Dobbin to do, Dobbin did what Dobbin did.

The procession headed up towards the hills flanked by the majestic Black Mountains that dominated the surrounding area and it was with immense satisfaction that Robert and I watched 'Roy Rogers' struggling to keep up with the rest of the group. As we admired the well-trained ponies that were now expertly treading the familiar but difficult path, we thanked the remaining staff for what had already been a brilliant day.

The afternoon came and thankfully so did a proper pony. They had obviously decided to take pity on me, and had plonked me on a magnificent beast. Sixteen hands high, chestnut in colour and bursting with raw pony power.

Now, correct me if I'm wrong but the front of a pony is the pointy bit, right, so why is all the noise coming from the rear? Blimey I've got a horse with an exhaust, I thought as we ambled slowly up the well-trodden path that led from the stables.

My guess is that a horse or pony can tell instantly the moment a rider gets on its back whether or not the jockey is a novice. Charger, as he was called, had immediately sussed me out and I spent the rest of the afternoon playing tug of war with the beast. Me yanking furiously at its reins trying to get his head up, only to be hauled headlong around his neck as he stretched as far as he could to eat the few tufts of grass that the other ponies had either missed or ignored.

When he did decide to move, it would be without warning, sending me hurtling backwards and only managing to stay on by grabbing the front of the saddle. I was completely losing my composure as I bounced up and down in the entirely opposite direction to that of the pony, jarring every bone in my pain-ridden arse.

The cubs however seemed to take this pony riding lark in their stride. They would gallop away at breakneck speed whenever the chance arose, all finding great amusement as their pony took a dump or when someone else's pony got a little excited at the mare in front. Even more fun was to be had by causing me to cringe with embarrassment as they asked stupid questions that they knew I wasn't going to answer. All in all the trip was a great success and as we drove back to camp our thoughts turned to the next activity Akela had arranged.

CHAPTER TWENTY TWO

As with most schools, fads and crazes would sweep the playground. These ranged from the Swiss Army knives some years before to electronic animals that needed feeding, exercising and baby sitting every four or five hours.

These 'must have' necessities that were cleverly forced from the pockets of long suffering parents by slick marketers would arrive at camp as trophies. Proudly displayed by the 'have's' and greatly envied by the 'have not's'.

Excluding the knives, all these were harmless enough, or so you may think. It was with fond memories and some surprise that the yo-yo returned to camp. In a world of high tech toys stretching the ever expanding imaginations of our future generations, this craze seemed just a little tame. Even Jonnie Boy here could relate to these and received some applause when I managed to get one to move up and down the string......twice!

Things move on and even the user-friendly yo-yo has advanced towards the twenty first century, thus allowing the player with very little practice to perform tricks that would amaze the smaller children, 'Around the World'

'Walking the Dog' 'Garrotte the Cub' and so on. Good clean harmless fun.

Michael, a pleasant young man who was employed by his father to help clean the school had come along to help. These keen young helpers were always welcome for reasons already explained

Being in the late teens is probably the worst time in our lives. A very difficult period of growing up. Desperately trying to find a balance between adulthood and childhood must at times, feel close to insanity.

Being unable to control your thoughts and mood swings causing shortfalls in your expected behaviour that never quite matches what you wanted, or wished to do, is to say the least confusing, and poor Michael was no exception.

His heart would tell him that he should be having fun, mixing in with the older boys who would follow him around in semi hero worship. These youngsters would hang on every word that the street-wise teenager would mumble, and in turn they would show him 'tricks' or loan him the latest yo-yo. His mind, however, would push towards the adults and the rewards of being treated as a grown up, never more so than when the drinks were being dispensed.

He managed to divide his time quite well, disappearing for long periods with the cubs, normally when there was work to be done, returning with a broad smile and a yo-yo when lunch or other goodies were on offer.

One of the small pleasures in what was always a hard week at camp was the reading of Sunday papers. This was allowed by Akela under the guise that it was vitally important to know what was going on in the world whilst we were out of touch, having been away for what was in fact one whole day. The hour's rest it granted was welcomed and as I settled down to scan 'The Times', all was well with my world.

A group of helpers gathered around Akela's tent enjoying the respite and sunshine that was such a premium in Wales, when Michael came bounding up a little bored and lost as to what to do. Unable to involve himself in meaningful adult conversation and reluctant to bury himself into one of the 'Sundays' he proceeded to practise his newly acquired skill on his well used and now, well worn yo-yo.

Some of the adults gathered as spectators with genuine interest in what Michael could do on this appendage that was now a permanent extension of his arm. "Show us what you can do, Mike," goaded Cathy for no other reason than to try and include him into the gathering.

"O.K how's this?" he bragged and promptly went into action.

"It's called 'Walking the Dog!'" announcing it's title like the showman all teenagers become when their egos are rubbed a little.

"And now 'The Cradle'" he beamed, growing in confidence as he built up to the finale of this spontaneous performance. In an effort to keep things going, he began pumping his arm harder and harder, trying to build up enough steam to complete the final trick.

"Around the World" he yelled, making sure he had everybody's attention.

Everybody's except mine of course, who was nose deep in the sports results, and promptly missed the part where he slung his arm skywards in a flurry of movement close to the speed of light. His mouth hung open as he witnessed the string fluttering slowly down towards the ground at a considerably lesser pace than when it went up. Its yo-yo less end now broken and frayed.

The audience stood in wonder, totally agog, eyes skyward.

The Reluctant Cub Scout

"Blimey that's clever," mused Robert. "Will it actually make it round the world?" he asked in faint amusement as he chuckled at the boy's expression. The rest watched in silence as the missile headed ever skyward, tracking its trajectory as if watching the latest space shuttle gracefully climb towards the stars and orbit. They returned to their conversations as the yo-yo disappeared completely, somewhere high above the clouds.

I was a good thirty feet away and could just make out a faint whistling noise coming from a skyward direction, a little south of where I was sitting.
Still oblivious to the drama that had just unfolded; I slowly turned the crumpled pages of the well read newspaper and basked in the warm Welsh sunshine grateful for the peace and quiet.

'Thwack'. Still travelling at considerable speed the yo-yo ricocheted off the top of my head, struck the ridge pole of the supply tent and landed unannounced into the dogs' water bowl sending plumes of ice cold water over the sleeping animals who were resting in the shade. The dogs were, by chance, tethered to one of the supporting legs of the chair I was sitting in. Yes, you guessed it.

Needless to say, Michael spent a little more time with the boys from then on. He kept well out of my reach, only asking on the odd occasions when we did manage to meet, if my head was all right.

"Fine," I would reply still trying to work out the odds of being hit on the head by some stupid yo-yo at cub camp. Michael, I mean, not the toy.

CHAPTER TWENTY THREE

We have a choice of two sites when we camp in Wales. The first is at Llanvair Discoed a few miles inland on the land owned by Richard Micklethwaite within spitting distance of the Severn Bridge. Our other venue is a small muddy field in close proximity to Hay-on-Wye. I was never sure who the landowner was but the site lies a mile or so from the pretty town that nestles on the banks of the crystal clear river from which it takes its name. It is probably most famous for its annual book fair, held exactly the same week as we were camping.

The journey from Camberley to Hay-on-Wye was arduous, taking well over four hours to reach our destination just a little north of the town. Akela felt that the local activities, surrounding mountains and beautiful countryside were enough to compensate for the long drive. Although I never really agreed, I looked forward to all the camps, and with this in mind I was happy to drive the minibus and prayed that after five exhausting days of camping I would manage to drive it back home safely without falling asleep. The distance from Lyndhurst school meant that we had no way of preparing the camp site prior to our arrival. Bearing in mind that this was now late May we would trust our luck to the elements and gamble that the weather would be kind to us, a fairly safe bet you would have thought!

Over the years we had been fairly lucky with the British weather. In early summer it rarely rains for very long and if it does, the sun is generally strong enough to dry the camp's contents, cubs and all, reasonably quickly. This could make life bearable at the worst of times if you understand my meaning........But not this time.

On our arrival we were staggered to find that the field allocated by our host for this year's cub camp, had up until then been used to graze herds of cattle. Through global warming or whoever is to blame, the previous winter had been the wettest on record and with the spring faring little better, these beasts of burden had managed to churn the entire field into a dung-filled quagmire.

The record-breaking weather was still on a roll. The rain had started to fall steadily as we squelched round the field looking for any sign of suitable land dry enough to pitch a tent. The boys sat in the steamed up minibus, drawing faces on the glass to deflect the boredom as Robert shook his head and squelched towards the huddle of adults who were reluctant to move for fear of disappearing into a turd filled hole.

"We can't stay here," he announced, totally pissed off by the lack of thought given by the farmer. "Come on, there's a barn over there. We'll shelter under that until we can sort this mess out."

At least the barn was dry. Smelly, but dry. The hay cut last summer had been neatly stacked to one side of the open ended building. This gave us ample space to drive the minibuses into the barn and park up. We disembarked the thirty or so disappointed cubs and surveyed our temporary shelter whilst Robert went off in search of the farmer and hopefully a more suitable campsite.

To alleviate the boredom the boys started to climb the mountains of hay that stood in bales four to five meters high, forcing tunnels between the large brick shaped bundles by wriggling into the cracks. Others built igloo shaped structures from the bales that were dislodged and would watch carefully as the large and heavy bales tumbled head over heels from the stack. They landed with huge clouds of chaff that hung in the air long enough to choke the adults before coating them in a film of farmyard dust.

From Mafeking to Molehills

All this activity had not surprisingly managed to disturb most of the inhabitants of this nice dry barn.

"Rats," screamed Akela.

"Look, hundreds of them," I shouted as I pointed at the flurry of wildlife as they scattered across the floor of the barn.

Panic ensued to say the least. The boys were yelping and jumping about not really sure of how dangerous these little furry animals were as they scampered under their hopping feet. Akela, Cathy and the others started a mad scramble as they fought for space on the bonnets of the minibuses. That left muggins as the only available 'Male' desperately trying to hold back the seething tide of rats as they bolted in panic in all directions, including the open doors of the minibuses.

Why is it always a man's job when it comes to catching rats? Why couldn't the Pied Piper have been a woman? The Pied Piperess of Hamlyn sounds pretty good to me. Thankfully Robert had returned just in time to witness the spectacle and after a few minutes of searching and shooing declared the minibuses safe for human habitation and was mildly amused at the speed with which we all embarked.

The Reluctant Cub Scout

The farmer, to his credit, had come up trumps, offering an alternative field that was as flat as your hat and self draining through a sub floor of the limestone that was common to these parts. The grass was short and as dry as one could expect and we quickly started to set up camp before the light faded. Not easy under these exceptional weather conditions.

The night was a long one, and we awoke to rain. Heavier then the previous day if that were possible, and we stared at the solid sky that told us that it was here to stay. Always the optimist Akela had nothing planned in the event of rain. Although a schedule for 'activities during rain' had been written, logged and sent to the Scouting Association's headquarters, nobody had actually believed we would have to revert to it and it had been left at home. We now had a whole day in front of us with little idea of how to keep our selves amused.

The morning was spent playing bingo and I had managed to drag this out for as long as possible, by inventing calls that made little sense such as six and two 'clickerty duck', 'on its own' forty three. The boys would shake their heads and mumble that I was mad. Having made sure that everybody had won at least one game each, I was grateful for the lull in the weather that allowed Akela to set up lunch and therefore break the tedium. There was no way we were going to keep the cubs happy all day playing bingo and with the cold and damp gnawing at our bones we opted for a trip to the town in the nice warm minibuses and a brisk walk round the shops.

Books, books, books, nothing but books. At any other time I would have willingly meandered around, blissfully happy whilst perusing the covers and turning the pages of literature in anticipation of their contents, but now was not the time.
"Where's the toy shop, Mister Laidlaw?"
"Where's the sweet shop, Mister Laidlaw?"
"Where's the toilet, Mister Laidlaw?"

"How do I know?" I would scream and with these harmonies continuously ringing in my ears I would trundle round the shops trying to dodge the rain, wishing for the first time in my camping life I was somewhere else.

On the Tuesday Akela had arranged that we travel down to the edge of town to a water adventure centre. The thought of getting wet didn't bother us anymore. By now we had seen enough of the stuff running down the back of our necks not to worry about a little thing like 'rapids.' Mercifully the rain had stopped and Robert and I spent a comfortable morning

The Reluctant Cub Scout

laying on the bank of the river as we watched the boys being trained in oarsman ship and the skills of moving in the direction of where you want to go rather than where you didn't. This idyllic scene and peaceful morning was punctuated only by the occasional bark of Robert shouting at the older boys to stop messing about and to pay attention. By lunchtime everybody was looking forward to the afternoon's adventure of wild water rafting through bubbling torrents and death defying rapids.

The chief instructor was a local man called Bruin. He had been plying his trade for some thirty odd years and was as relaxed as anybody I had ever met. His chubby smiling face heavily creased by the years gave a kind but weathered expression and was surrounded by locks of unkempt hair that had been bleached bright white by the sun. With his softly spoken tones and gentle manner the children immediately warmed to him, all listening intently as this old sea dog whispered his instructions.

The 'rafts' were actually two aluminium Canadian canoes 'Hiawatha' style strapped together side by side for safety thus making them almost unsinkable. Each canoe took four people, making eight passengers per raft.

From Mafeking to Molehills

By the time the inevitable swapping about and squabbles had finished, Cathy and I were the only two left that hadn't got a boat.

"Hang on a bit. I'll get another," said the ever-helpful Bruin and duly disappeared into the adjacent car park across the road. Five minutes later he returned with a very dubious looking canoe battered by years of abuse balanced on his head, a pair of worm eaten paddles and a couple of tatty looking life jackets tucked under his nicely tanned arms. Here we go again, Jonny and the short straw.

In front of an appreciative audience I managed to steady the canoe long enough to allow the now petrified Cathy to board. The boat was rocking as she swayed in harmony with the wobbly bits that were displayed through her skin tight - and I mean skin tight - Lycra outfit that was more of a fashion statement than a practical piece of clothing. But the instructors seemed to enjoy the view as she gingerly sat aboard the canoe.

I managed to keep my balance long enough to push off from the side and with a little help from one of the paddles headed off in roughly the same direction as the now disappearing armada. Useless, absolutely useless! Having been omitted from the morning's lessons on how to steer a boat, Cathy and I just went round and round in circles. The more I paddled the more she wobbled, the more she wobbled the more I lost my concentration. Robert, never one to miss an opportunity, was by this time standing on the bank clicking away with his camera. I could hear his giggles from mid stream as he waved us off with one hand whilst wiping the tears away with the other.

Bruin, bless him, ever mindful of his responsibilities, had turned back and paddled the half mile or so against the strong current to rescue us. He slung a line and shouted at the now hysterical Cathy to attach it to the bow of our motionless vessel. Cathy just looked at him.
"The front of the canoe you daft mare," he sighed looking at the clueless pair already soaked by my inadequate attempts at rowing. He then turned and promptly towed us towards the others whilst shouting instructions at me on how to steer and propel the craft properly. With consummate ease that only confirmed how out of my depth I was, he towed us at speed towards the flotilla of cubs and released us to our fate.

My embarrassment was compounded by the fact that the boys were mastering their rafts with expertise. Most of them managed to splash me every time they paddled past, all without missing a beat as they raced each other to the next set of rapids. Well, a gentle trickle of shallow water flowing over nice smooth rocks was probably a better description. But it made the water churn white and was fast enough for Cathy and I to scream as we clung on to the side for dear life letting the canoe follow the current that guided us through the torrents of foaming water like some fairground ride.

After an hour I had slowly mastered the steering. Even Cathy managed to contribute to the paddling as she grew in confidence safe in the knowledge that even if I was stupid enough to sink us both, the water was so refreshingly clean and shallow that it wouldn't be such a bad experience if we were to capsize. And of course there was always Bruin to save her!

With the sun beating down we made good headway. Making occasional use of the paddle we meandered slowly along with the drifting flow as it carried us past the lush green vegetation that draws life from the cool waters and flourishes in abundance on the rich dark soil that forms the shores of the Wye. As we continued downstream the banks would steadily encroach upon the water, drawing the silver birch and weeping willows ever closer. Eventually the channel would narrow forcing the traffic into single file before slowly widening and making another turn towards Chepstow.

Like silent hunters they stood and waited. Ready to maul the unwelcome intruder that has dared to enter their world. They held their victims just long enough to paw them with stringy golden tendrils as if tasting for food. Feeling their prey as they brushed the skin that passed these landlocked monsters. We turned our heads sharply and ducked from the reach of their spindly fingers as we fended ourselves from their spidery grasp. Turning as we made our escape to witness the trees hurriedly resetting their traps before another unsuspecting victim paddled past.

The only blot on this picturesque scene was the rotting carcass of a deer that had managed to drown itself a couple of days beforehand. This was now so bloated with gases that it effortlessly sailed passed us with its legs in the air as if it were some tourist floating about on the Dead Sea, its stomach bulging fit to burst as it span grotesquely with the currents.

" O look, someone's killed Bambi," shouted one of the older boys as he poked it with his oar sending it gyrating off towards the bank and laughed as he watched it snag on the branch of an over hanging tree.

From Mafeking to Molehills

"That's it, spoil a good view," I said as we stared at the carcass as it managed to break away from its restraints, puncturing itself just under the water line with a large enough hole to allow it to propel itself 'motor boat' style towards Cathy and I.

I had to forcibly restrain her from abandoning ship as it putted past the boys who by now were rolling about with laughter before it bumped into us, nicely snagging itself about amidships. Gagging from the smell I frantically prodded the beast in the vain hope that I might be able to free it so that it could continue on its final journey in peace. Fat chance, all I managed to do was loose an oar as it lodged tightly into the rotting carcass, releasing what was left of the decomposing gasses. With the weight of the oar it spun upright so that the head was now poking out of the water. Its black, empty eye sockets stared blindly at me as it sank.

After what seemed a suitably long enough period of mourning we proceeded with the journey. Luckily there were no more incidents as we headed to our meeting point where Robert and Akela had brought the minibuses to transport us back to camp.

The Reluctant Cub Scout

Out of the four days we camped at Hay on Wye the rain stopped long enough for us to climb into the canoes, paddle down the river, sink the deer and climb out again before returning to fall in a relentless downpour. By Wednesday we'd given up. We drove the boy's home late that night much to the relief of their parents, who by now had been listening to the weather forecast and knew we were getting wet. We were reluctant to abandon camp and had never in the fifteen years of camping even been close to doing so. But to make them endure another miserable night was not on. After all, this was meant to be fun and it wasn't. Thankfully we never went back to Wales.

EPILOGUE

In early November 2001 Akela was awarded the Order of Merit. The award was granted by the Scouting Association for her service, diligence and hard work.

Nobody deserved this acknowledgement more than she did.

As Robert and Akela look towards the horizon of retirement, they should take with them the comfort and knowledge that many hundreds of Cub Scouts are grateful for the time and experience they have given.

I still turn up every Thursday eager for my weekly dose of escapism, always grateful for the fortification of laughter. It is a sad fact that one day boys will no longer attend cubs because it isn't fashionable anymore, or because the scout movement no longer has the support of the necessary volunteers and leaders.

The truth is that within our modern world, society frowns upon adults, especially grown men, wanting to be involved with other people's children. Having spoken to many parents over the years the question they always seem to ask is why I do it.

The Reluctant Cub Scout

Maybe if they were volunteered into spending just a few days with their children, larking about in a muddy field with torrential rain running down the back of their necks, freezing cold, tired, sore and hungry, they would understand.

Or maybe not....

From Mafeking to Molehills

The Reluctant Cub Scout

From Mafeking to Molehills

The Reluctant Cub Scout

From Mafeking to Molehills